"Hi there, friend.*"*

David's words were spoken in a tone that stroked along Jenny's nerve ends like the tender-rough lick of a kitten's tongue. It took the length of several erratic heartbeats for their gazes to disentangle and for Jenny to notice the single, yellow rosebud he held out to her.

"It's from my own garden," he said, taking her hand and putting the rose in it. "When I picked it, it occurred to me how much the two of you are alike."

"Oh?" The note of teasing in his voice raised Jenny's guard. "And how's that?"

"Two long-stemmed beauties . . . with thorns."

"Oh." Jenny could handle that. She ran a finger over the stem. "No thorns here."

"That's because I removed them."

The look that accompanied that statement was too smug for Jenny to ignore. "If you think you can remove *my* thorns next, David Waterman, you're in the wrong garden."

Dear Reader,

It's March—and spring is just around the corner. We all know spring is the season of love, but at Silhouette Romance, every season is romantic, and every month we offer six heartwarming stories that capture the laughter, the tears, the sheer joy of falling in love. This month is no exception!

Honey, I'm Home by Rena McKay is a delightful reminder that even the most dashing hero is a little boy at heart, and Lindsay Longford's *Pete's Dragon* will reaffirm your belief in the healing power of love . . . and make-believe. The intense passion of Suzanne Carey's *Navajo Wedding* will keep you spellbound, the sizzling *Two To Tango* by Kristina Logan will quite simply make you want to dance, and Linda Varner's *As Sweet as Candy* will utterly charm you.

No month is complete without our special WRITTEN IN THE STARS selection. This month we have the exciting, challenging Pisces man in Anne Peters's *Storky Jones Is Back in Town*.

Throughout the year we'll be publishing stories of love by all your favorite Silhouette Romance authors—Diana Palmer, Suzanne Carey, Annette Broadrick, Brittany Young and many, many more. The Silhouette Romance authors and editors love to hear from readers, and we'd love to hear from *you!*

Happy Reading!

Valerie Susan Hayward
Senior Editor

ANNE PETERS

Storky Jones Is Back in Town

Silhouette Romance

Published by Silhouette Books New York

America's Publisher of Contemporary Romance

To Debbie Petersen, who is not only a terrific wife,
mother and private pilot, but a wonderful daughter, as well.
Love you, Deb. Thanks for the technical advice, and for
your unfailing and continuous support of my writing.

SILHOUETTE BOOKS
300 E. 42nd St., New York, N.Y. 10017

STORKY JONES IS BACK IN TOWN

Copyright © 1992 by Anne Hansen

LOVE AND THE PISCES MAN
Copyright © 1992 by Harlequin Enterprises B.V.

ISBN: 0-373-08850-7

First Silhouette Books printing March 1992

All the characters in this book have no existence outside the
imagination of the author and have no relation whatsoever to
anyone bearing the same name or names. They are not even
distantly inspired by any individual known or unknown to the
author, and all incidents are pure invention.

®: Trademark used under license and registered in the United
States Patent and Trademark Office and in other countries.

Printed in the U.S.A.

Books by Anne Peters

Silhouette Romance

Through Thick and Thin #739
Next Stop: Marriage #803
And Daddy Makes Three #821
Storky Jones Is Back in Town #850

Silhouette Desire

Like Wildfire #497

ANNE PETERS

Astrologically speaking, Anne Peters is the only mammal in her immediate family. She is an Aries, while everyone else is either Cancer or Pisces. As a consequence, she has firsthand knowledge that these purportedly "cold-blooded" creatures are anything but cold-blooded. And scientific data to the contrary, electric eels are *not* the only aquatic critters to generate sparks! Other than that, Anne's belief in the signs of the zodiac, in almanacs and horoscopes tends to be absolute: favorable aspects and predictions are absolutely believed, while those that are unfavorable are just as absolutely dismissed.

PISCES

Twelfth sign of the Zodiac
February 20 to March 20
Symbol: Fish
Planet: Jupiter
Element: Water
Stone: Aquamarine
Color: Green, Purple
Metal: Platinum
Flower: Jonquil
Lucky Day: Thursday
Countries: Portugal, Egypt, Southern Asia
Cities: Alexandria, Seville

Famous Pisceans

Michelangelo
Albert Einstein
Jerry Lewis
Nat "King" Cole

Elizabeth Taylor
Liza Minelli
Jennifer Jones
Merle Oberon

★

Chapter One

" . . . But to suggest, as numerous articles have, that in this day and age a single woman of thirty and up is, quote, on the shelf, unquote, is well..." The woman speaker paused, then added with a small laugh of exasperation, "Preposterous, is what it is."

The woman's laugh, throaty with a husky sexiness, rather than her statement was what caught David Waterman's attention. Up until then the dialogue emanating from his television set had been nothing more than background babble, listened to with one ear as his brain barely chugged along on autopilot while he waited for his coffee and the morning news.

Now, however, he froze in the act of stepping into his undershorts. His head swiveled toward the TV, and vague disquiet instantly ballooned into one gigantic mess of contradictory emotions as his eyes homed in on the attractive blonde on the screen.

Good *God,* he thought. Guilt and remorse, both as familiar as old shoes though not nearly as comfortable, swiftly joined his initial shock and totally eclipsed a fleeting surge of pleasure and affection.

Storky Jones!

She was saying, "Just because the nineties woman has many more options available to her than her mother had, and just because she might *choose* to exercise those options in a myriad of ways other than matrimony, there are those—males, of course—who maintain it is rejection rather than choice which has kept us from the altar."

David stared at the TV, suddenly feeling twice his thirty-two years old. He grimly pulled on his shorts and, without taking his eyes off the set for even a blink, dropped down on the edge of the bed.

Jenny Jones!

He sat with his hands dangling between spread knees and watched humor brighten her navy blue eyes to sapphire. Hearing again her husky laugh, his breath got trapped somewhere in midchest.

"Do you know that, statistically, married men are the only group of people who perceive themselves as happier than single professional women?" she demanded of her audience. Her neat brows arched. "And why not, right? They have it all, don't they? Fulfilling careers *and,* more often than not, at home the little woman ready to soothe their weary brow even as she juggles a multitude of other responsibilities which usually include a full-time job."

As applause and appreciative laughter followed, David studied the animated image on the screen in minute detail. He took in the light dusting of freckles across the bridge of her nose, the generous mouth curved in a cheeky smile, the sparkling eyes. Large, and as soft and blue as pansies, they had always been—to him—her most attractive feature.

Not that he ever would have let her guess there was anything about her he found even remotely interesting. Quite the contrary.

The camera shot widened to include Georgette Myerson, who hosted Seattle's popular early-morning program *Timely Topics.* Aware of the minutes ticking by, David got up off the bed with a sigh. He knew and admired the beautiful Georgette, had even taken her out a time or two, but today his attention remained exclusively on her guest.

He padded to the dresser, got a pair of socks out of one drawer, a shirt out of another and proceeded to get dressed.

Amid the sustained applause, a self-conscious flush began to visibly heighten the color of Jenny's cheeks, and just as it invariably had in the past, this tiny chink in her armor called forth in David a surge of grudging tenderness. If she could blush like that, he thought, then surely the trappings of severity and sophistication—her tumble of honey-blond hair somehow tortured into sleek submission, the no-nonsense, don't-touch-me suit and high-collared shirt—were still just that: trappings.

Georgette's image now filled the screen. "For those of you who've just tuned in," she said, "this is the tail end of segment three of our five-part discussion of issues concerning today's woman. Our guest today is Eugenie Jones. A successful translator and interpreter, Jenny has returned to the Pacific Northwest after ten years back east and abroad. She is, by her own admission, thirty-two years old and contentedly single."

As the shot once again widened to include Jenny, as well as the living room arrangement that was the *Timely Topics* set, David stepped into tan slacks and, scowling, wondered what the hell *contentedly single* meant.

"You're back in Seattle to stay, I presume?" Georgette was asking.

"I certainly am."

Jenny crossed her legs, drawing David's glance to the motion. There always had been miles and miles of legs on her, he recalled, but had they been such shapely miles?

"Several months ago, I opened my own business here, as a matter of fact."

"Wonderful," Georgette enthused, adding to someone off camera, "Almost time?" She turned back to Jenny. "I'm told we've got about half a minute to get in a plug."

"Thanks." Jenny faced front. "We're Multi-Lingual Services, Inc., and we do both business and literary translations in Spanish, French, German, Russian and Japanese."

"*You* speak all of those languages?"

"Heavens no. I only speak German, French and Spanish."

"*Only,*" Georgette interjected as an aside with a comic rolling of the eyes. "Some of us barely manage in English, isn't that right, people?"

Jenny chuckled along with the audience as she added, "Well, we have two part-timers on staff who manage just great in several other languages, and they'd be glad to work full-time."

"Hear that, everybody?" Georgette called out as the theme song heralded the end of the show. "Give Multi-Lingual Services a call if there's anything you need translated, and let's have a nice round of applause for our talented guest."

Credits now partially obliterated a shot of the two women, one blond, tall and reed slender, one short, dark and curvacious. Both were on their feet and applauding along with the almost exclusively female audience.

"Do you do interpreting, too?" Georgette's voice was fading.

"Yes..."

Fade-out. End. Cut to network logo and jingle. Commercial break. "Washaway, Washaway, Moms just love fresh Washaway..."

No longer in the mood even for the news, David switched off the set but continued to stare at it for long moments. He was deep in thought. Storky Jones was back in town. His mind was arguing with his heart, his conscience, both of which were urging him to do something. Look up her number and call her. Maybe take her to lunch.

But his mind balked. Let sleeping dogs lie, old son. What'll it change, your going to see her? Think she'll like you any better than she ever did?

David's jaw tightened. Hardly.

Jenny was in her favorite position. Shoes and jacket off, legs dangling over one armrest of the high-backed swivel chair fronting her desk, torso draped serpentine fashion into its cushiony depth, nose buried in a book. Countless were the hours her mother had found her thus, and countless had been the lectures on curvature of the spine, unladylike deportment, etc., etc., all of which had, for the most part, fallen on deaf ears.

Collar open, a pencil clamped between her teeth, Jenny was reading—or, rather, trying to read and comprehend—a novel by an up-and-coming German author, in German, preparatory to translating it into English. For the tenth time in as many minutes, she lowered the book. A sigh, more like a groan, escaped past the pencil. The story was impossible to follow. The plot, if there was one, was buried in long-winded prose and disjointed gibberish mouthed by seemingly crazed characters. Avant-garde literature, the publisher had called it. Jenny shook her head and tried to concentrate once more on the printed page. Who read this stuff?

The purring of the phone moments later brought another respite. Jenny let the book drop into her lap and combined a lusty yawn and stretch with the picking up of the receiver.

"Yes, Ruth?"

"Did I wake you?" Ruth Franklin, Jenny's middle-aged office manager cum secretary asked dryly.

"Heck, no." Another yawn mingled with Jenny's light laugh. "I wasn't sleeping, just somewhat comatose from this...this *tome* I'm supposed to translate for Universal Publishing."

"Bad, huh?"

"Worse. A legal contract in Swahili'd be easier to follow."

"You don't speak Swahili."

"Precisely."

They shared a chuckle, then Ruth said, "Mr. Shafer is on line three."

"Thanks." Jenny punched the necessary button. "Bill! I'm glad you called. Did you catch the show this morning?"

"I did."

"Well?"

"She's very lovely."

"And *nice,* Bill." Jenny swung her legs off the chair and sat up straight to better make her point. "That's much more important here. Georgette Myerson is genuinely nice. You'll love her."

She pulled a face at the heavy sigh that was William Shafer III's only response to her enthusiasm. "She's eager to do this, Bill," she pressed. "And you did agree...."

"I know." Another sigh. "How did I ever let that woman talk me into entering this bachelor auction, anyway?"

"'That woman,' as you put it, is your sister, that's why. And you love her."

"Humph. Afraid of her, more like."

"Yes, well." Jenny grinned. Bill Shafer had become a dear friend in the four months since he'd first come to her with *The Complete Works of Goethe,* a prized first edition, in the original German. He was, at forty-three, a shy, scholarly man, and the two of them had discovered almost immediately that they were kindred souls.

Jenny too loved books and quiet times. And had had to come to terms with less than conventional looks. To paraphrase the never-forgotten descriptions of one David Waterman, she was built straight up and down like a coat tree; she was a stork, a bean pole. And her ears stood out like pitcher handles.

She'd had the ears fixed a few years ago, but there hadn't been a heck of a lot she'd been able to do about being five foot ten except to stand proud. Which she had done and still did.

While she was tall, however, Bill Shafer was short. Too short, in his opinion, which Jenny had often told him was ridiculous. Too short for what? For whom?

Women liked taller men, he'd confided one night over dinner and a companionable bottle of wine at Jenny's apartment. Women liked *physical* men, aggressive, macho men.

Not so, not every woman, Jenny had protested, recalling her own intense dislike of David Waterman, who even at eighteen had been physical, aggressive and macho as all get out. But she could see Bill's point. Most of the seniors in high school and the majority of coeds in college had come running—scratch that, *panting*—any time David had crooked a finger in their direction. And, boy, had he crooked....

Suddenly aware that her thoughts were straying, Jenny stifled a sigh of self annoyance and snapped her mind back to the task of shoring up Bill Shafer's shaky self-esteem.

"Not every woman is after your money, Bill," she assured him. The William Shafers I and II had, respectively, launched and expanded into an empire a very lucrative chain of drugstores, leaving the third William in the unenviable position of having extreme wealth but neither a head for, nor interest in, business. Which was how he had become a philanthropist, a collector of rare books, and a very lonely man.

Jenny was glad that he'd also become her friend. "*I'm* not," she added. "After your money."

"I know." A glum sigh. "But you're different."

"Well, so is Georgette," Jenny said decisively. "What's more, apart from being extremely successful in her own right, she comes from quite a wealthy family herself."

"Myerson?" There followed a lengthy silence as Bill mused.

"The L.A. Myersons," Jenny supplied helpfully.

"Hmm."

He'd never heard of them, Jenny surmised. But then that wasn't surprising since she'd just made them up. Anything to make him receptive to Georgette who, on learning that Jenny was a friend of Bill Shafer's, had confided that she'd been attracted to him ever since she'd glimpsed him at a benefit reception for the Seattle Opera.

Attractive shorter men were hard to find, she'd told Jenny, and being merely five foot nothing herself and no shrinking violet, she had admitted to resenting the fact that her tall dates tended to eclipse her. Couldn't Jenny introduce her to Bill?

Jenny had met Georgette shortly after arriving back in Seattle. They were both members of Soroptimist International, an organization of professional and business women devoted to good works in the community. In the months that followed they'd become good friends. In trying to come up with a way of bringing Bill and Georgette together without spooking Bill, Jenny decided the bachelor auction the club was planning to put on as a benefit for homeless children would be perfect.

Bill's sister, Dr. Jane Montgomery, was another member of Soroptimist as well as chair of the Bachelor Committee. She and her committee members were in charge of lining up eligible bachelors willing to donate two evenings of their time for a good cause—one evening for the auction itself, and one for the date they'd have to go on with the successful bidder. It went without saying that Jane wouldn't take no for an answer from her only brother. After all, not only was he a bachelor, he was also one of Seattle's leading citizens. It behooved him to set a good example for others in the community.

She also thought Jenny's plan for introducing Bill to Georgette quite wonderful.

Some two weeks later, Jenny cast one last glance at herself in the full-length mirror on the back of her bedroom door and pronounced herself passably chic. She hurried to answer the doorbell. Georgette lived in the penthouse of the same building as Jenny in the Seattle suburb of Bellevue, and they were sharing a cab.

Stunning in a flowing tunic over formfitting black leather pants, Georgette gave Jenny's rather more conservative, yet flattering, teal silk shirtwaist a quick perusal.

She crinkled her nose. "I swear you svelte and long-stemmed model types could wear potato sacking and still look sensational. I hate you."

Jenny, unoffended, laughed. "I take it you don't like my dress."

"Ordinarily no, but on you it looks good. On me..." Georgette shuddered, then pirouetted. "What do you think, Jen—is this too gypsyish?"

"You'll put every woman at that auction to shame and you know it," Jenny told her, picking her tiny handbag up off the Korean chest in her entry. "Ready if you are."

"What *I* am is nervous." Georgette countered Jenny's look of skepticism with an affronted toss of the head. "I'm human."

"Well, so's Bill Shafer," Jenny assured her. "Very much so. Which is why he needs you to be strong."

"I suppose."

"The taxi's waiting, meter running...." Jenny herded Georgette out the door, down the stairs and into the cab. "I just hope there's someone even remotely interesting for *me* to bid on tonight," she said.

"Honestly, Jen, only you could doubt that there would be." Georgette slanted her a look of patent disgust. "I mean, every male who is *anybody* in this town will be strutting his stuff on that stage tonight. If you can't find one to bid on in that crowd, my darling, you've got a problem."

Jenny sniffed. "So I'm choosy."

"What you *are* is ridiculous," Georgette retorted. "You don't actually believe that 'contentedly single' garbage you spouted on my show, do you? God, I hope not," she answered, and Jenny dryly surmised the question must have been a rhetorical one. "Me, I'd give just about anything to be married."

She fell silent, staring out of her window. Jenny, for lack of anything to say in rebuttal, did likewise. After a lengthy silence, Georgette turned to her. "Well, do you?" she demanded. "Believe it, I mean?"

Did she? Jenny gave it some thought and came to the happy conclusion that, most of the time, she did. Sure, there were times when she thought of Russell and wondered what might have been if he had lived. Would they really have gone ahead and gotten married, as they'd always planned?

Jenny withdrew from the question as she usually did. After all, who could say what might have been? The fact was, Russell was dead and so was the past. She, on the other hand, was alive and had made a good life for herself. A life that fulfilled and contented her. What else could anyone ask?

She smiled at Georgette. "As a matter of fact," she said, "I do believe that garbage."

Georgette rolled her eyes. "And I don't believe *you* for a minute, but I suppose that's neither here nor there."

They pursued their own thoughts the rest of the way and arrived at the prestigious Fairview Hotel along with throngs of other women. Most of them were of about the same age and status as Georgette and Jenny. Professional women of comfortable means: upwardly mobile, supremely confident—on the surface, at least—and passionately independent.

Yet, Jenny reflected with considerable amusement, here we all are, dressed to the gills and assembled for the sole purpose of ogling, judging and acquiring *A Man!* No doubt, behavioral scientists could have a field day with an event like this.

Jenny and Georgette were sort of swept along into the hotel's lavish foyer with other arrivals. They stood in line to check their coats and to register for the auction. They were told the rules: Bidding to start at fifty dollars, to be raised by ten-dollar increments with a ceiling bid of three hundred dollars. Tax deductible, of course.

"Three hundred dollars!" Jenny shook her head in disbelief. "Believe me, Georgette, deductible or not, the man would have to be *some* paragon for me to ever part with that kind of money!"

"Hmm." Georgette was scanning the crowd. "Do you suppose they let the bachelors mingle before the event?"

"I doubt it." Jenny, not really caring one way or another, cast only a cursory look around. She caught the eye of a couple of women she knew. They beckoned her toward the ballroom. With a nod of comprehension in their direction, she touched Georgette's elbow.

"Babs Wood and Sheila Laughlin want us to join them inside. The thing won't start for about forty-five minutes. We can have a glass of wine or something. Maybe get a table near the stage and runway."

"Good idea."

Jenny led the way into the ballroom and to a large round table near the stage from where Sheila was frantically waving to them. Several other women, some of them acquaintances, were already seated there and ordering drinks from the hovering waiters. The room was humming with conversation punctuated by bursts of laughter and shrieks of recognition as old friends met. A combination of cigarette smoke and expensive perfume gave the air a heavy quality that Jenny feared would make her head ache before the night was over.

Jenny and Georgette greeted the table's other occupants, exchanging introductions with those they had not met before at Soroptimist club meetings and the like. Their faces alight with anticipation, the women were discussing the pros and cons of the various bachelors whose names, ages and occupations were listed alphabetically in the program. They radiated such palpable excitement, Jenny couldn't help but be at least a little infected by it.

She took a seat, ordered a glass of wine and picked up her own program. Like the others, she studied the names and brief biographies with interest. The lineup was certainly impressive.

Roy Emerson, she read. Thirty-eight years old. Attorney.

Ernest H. Kingsley. Forty-five. Businessman. Now *him* Jenny knew something about. She'd met him at some function or other shortly after returning to Seattle and, since he'd seemed charming and witty, had accepted a date with him. What a mistake. The man had been all over her like a bad rash before they'd even left Jenny's apartment. Pity the woman who bid on *him*.

Jenny read on. Richard T. ("Artee") Rawlins. Thirty-five. Disc jockey at—

"Look at this, Jen." Georgette leaned over to poke her finger at Bill Shafer's bio. "He's listed as an entrepreneur and philanthropist. I love it."

"Hmm." Jenny listened with only half an ear as Georgette almost reverently read aloud the rest of Bill's familiar biography. Her own gaze had scooted past Georgette's finger to the second-to-last name on the page. It was the name of the man she'd hoped never to have to lay eyes on again, and it all but leaped off the page and grabbed her: David Waterman. Thirty-two. Waterman Aviation...

Jenny knew a brief, cowardly urge to get up and run. If there was one man she didn't wish to see, or be seen by, it was David Waterman. Only with difficulty did her saner side prevail. Hadn't it been ten years since they'd last been face-to-face? That was a long time, a time during which she had changed. She was no longer either awkward or introverted. The David Watermans of the world no longer had the power to intimidate or upset her.

And, anyway, she was just one face in hundreds here tonight. He wouldn't even notice her.

"I think I'll go for the deejay," she told Georgette, abruptly flipping back to the page with Rawlins's name on it.

"He's all right."

"You've gone out with him?"

"Oh, sure," Georgette replied absently, "but before you decide—" she slid her finger down to the *W*s "—I beg you to look at this guy, David Waterman. I think he'd be perfect for you." Contemplating the name, she heaved a sigh of regret. "If he weren't so darn tall, I might've tried harder to land him myself. We've dated, you know," she added unnecessarily for Jenny's benefit.

"Of course you have."

Jenny's dry tone and the grimace that accompanied her rejoinder visibly took Georgette aback. "What's that supposed to mean?" she asked, bristling.

"Means if there's anyone in skirts left in Seattle who hasn't dated David Waterman, I'd be most surprised."

Georgette blinked. "You know him?"

"*Knew* him, if you please." Jenny slapped the program onto the table, facedown. "And I'd like to keep it in the past tense, thank you very much."

"Such hostility." Georgette eyed her with undisguised speculation. "What'd he do, stand you up at the senior prom?"

"No, but he did manage to ruin it for me. Along with many other occasions, I might add."

"Sounds intriguing. Do tell me more...."

"Ladies!"

Jenny blessed the emcee's timely bid for attention. Georgette's reputation as a crack interviewer was well earned, she had a knack for getting people to broadcast their innermost secrets. For now, at least, Jenny's were safe.

"Good evening, ladies," the master of ceremonies called above the slowly abating hubbub, adding, "I was going to say 'and gentlemen,' but there aren't any, are there? Except backstage, of course."

Jenny joined in the burst of laughter, though more as a release from tension than out of appreciation for the man's sluggish humor.

"With the fine crop of bachelors Seattle has to offer," he went on to proclaim, "their desirability is exceeded only by the beauty of the assembled ladies."

"Wait'll the bidding starts," Georgette whispered into Jenny's ear. "He won't think we're ladies then."

They exchanged grins, then listened as the emcee went on to mention the charity they were all there to support that evening. He thanked the many volunteers whose diligence had made the event possible, and ended his soliloquy with a not very original, "Let the show begin!"

The applause was thunderous, even interspersed with whistles and catcalls. The cacophony subsided somewhat when the first bachelor's name was called.

Prepared to just sit back and enjoy the show until it was Rawlins's turn, Jenny was not a little surprised to hear, "Dustin J. MacPherson!"

So the men weren't sent out in alphabetical order. All right. Jenny sat up straighter and joined the applause. She'd better pay attention then.

Mr. MacPherson, dapper in a pin-striped suit and gleaming shoes but looking a little apprehensive, crossed the stage and marched down the runway like a soldier on

parade. At its end he jerked a stiff little bow and marched
back to stand center stage while the first bid rang out.

"Fifty dollars."

"Sixty."

"Seventy . . ."

Dustin "sold" for eighty dollars, and the successful
bidder was told that she could pay for and meet with her
"prize" backstage, after the show.

"Dolly Grimes has been lusting after poor Dustin for
months," Georgette said to Jenny, "but he's always managed to elude her. Seems like his luck's run out."

Jenny shot her a repressive glance but couldn't quite
stifle a snicker. "You're terrible."

"I know."

"William X. Shafer III!"

Georgette's unrepentant grin faded. "Oh my gosh, there
he is. One hundred dollars!" To the delight of the crowd
and Jenny, she was on her feet and bidding before Bill had
even reached the start of the runway.

He stopped walking to squint her way, and Jenny could
only sit in wonder as, on making eye contact with Georgette, she watched a breathtaking smile blossom on his
face, transforming it from merely pleasant to downright
handsome.

Beside her, Georgette gasped and pressed folded hands
to her bosom. "I'm in love," she murmured, and stood
entranced as the man of her dreams belatedly recalled
himself and slowly walked down the runway. Several bids
were called while she just stood there, mute, and it took a
strategic jab of Jenny's elbow to bring home to her the fact
that someone else might well snatch her prince if she didn't
look lively.

"Two hundred dollars."

Jenny crossed fingers on both hands for luck, which seemed to help. Into the lengthy silence, the emcee called, "Sold for two hundred dollars to Ms. Georgette Myerson! Mr. Shafer, you're a lucky man."

Bill's besotted expression visibly seconded that statement as he left the stage. Ecstatic, Jenny and Georgette hugged.

"We did it! Oh, Jen, did you see...?"

Jenny gladly endured her friend's enthusiastic monologue while several other bachelors came and went. She just knew that romance would blossom for Bill and Georgette. On the surface it might seem that they had nothing in common, but, in fact, they were like two sides of the same coin. Georgette's gregariousness was the perfect counterpart to Bill's reticence. She would draw him out, liven him up, while he would calm her, soften and mellow her....

"David Waterman!"

Jenny was jolted by the name as if by a charge of electricity. For no reason at all, her heart began to beat so hard she might have been running uphill at full speed rather than quietly sitting. She no longer heard a word Georgette was saying, nor the thunderous applause and whistles of the audience.

She sat breathless, her eyes riveted to the curtain through which, with the negligent grace of a predator, strode the nemesis of her youth and Russell Dalton's best friend.

Chapter Two

David saw Jenny the moment he stepped out from behind the curtain. Wide-eyed and ramrod straight, she sat staring at him. He could detect neither warmth nor encouragement in her fixed regard but let his gaze connect with hers anyway.

He sauntered out onto the stage with all the cocky brashness he'd worked so hard as a kid to cultivate, but the truth was his knees were shaking. He'd much rather be flying a plane blindfolded through a thunderstorm than stand in front of this throng of clamoring females. He knew a goodly number of them, had dated more than his share in his wilder, not-so-distant past. Nice women, most of them professional or business types. Decent, attractive, hardworking.

But by the looks and sound of them now, apparently ready to tear his clothes off.

Summoning a confident smile, he kept his eyes on Jenny's for as long as possible. As the bidding went hot and heavy and he made his way across the stage toward the runway, she remained unmoving, indifferent. He was surprised by how much this bothered him, he'd thought that he'd long ago reconciled himself to the fact that in Storky Jones's opinion he was lower than a snake.

A gladiator with the intelligence of an amoeba, she'd once told him he was. A mental midget, a jock—all brawn and no brain. Of course he'd probably razzed her pretty good first, for her to get so mad.

His plastic smile widened, became natural, lighting his eyes with rueful humor. They'd sure been something, those verbal free-for-alls of theirs. And poor old Russ, caught in the middle, always the diplomat trying to make peace....

David paused at the end of the runway to throw kisses, bestow some winks, play the crowd. Hell, he was here for one reason only: to fetch as much money as possible for those homeless kids. If that meant playing the part everyone seemed to expect him to play, then play it he would. Nobody needed to know what went on inside him, nobody needed to know it took the replaying of long-ago fireworks between himself and the only woman in the room who wasn't hollering and laughing to keep his step jaunty and his smile bold.

Turning, he started back up the runway, and his gaze latched onto Jenny's again.

"Two hundred and eighty dollars," the auctioneer was shouting. "Who'll give me two hundred and ninety?"

"Over here!"

"Two hundred and ninety, ladies! The bid for the handsome Mr. Waterman is two hundred and ninety dollars, do I hear three hundred?"

The sudden silence was deafening as the women balked at going that one extra mile to the limit. None of the candidates so far that evening had brought in the highest allowable bid.

"Three hundred!"

Pandemonium erupted. The auctioneer uselessly banged his gavel. Georgette was jumping up and down and pounding Jenny on the shoulder.

David stood unmoving, center stage.

Jenny sat like a rock in a tempest, hearing nothing, feeling nothing, trapped in the bright intensity of David Waterman's relentless gaze like a rabbit in the headlights of a car.

Nothing had prepared her for the reality of him after all these years. He was no longer just a cocksure young stud with flashy good looks and a what-the-hell smile. The smile was still there, but it seemed to her mellower and tinged with self-directed humor. He looked so good up there on that stage. Tall and straight, with the kind of figure designers dreamed of when creating tuxedos. The set of his shoulders, the tilt of his head, his walk—all of those things underscored the impression that here was a man who was confident without taking himself too seriously.

None of those things made Jenny like him any better, and yet...

"Sold for three hundred dollars to the lovely lady in green. Stand up and be recognized by the envious multitudes, fair lady," she heard the emcee pompously announce.

Georgette was madly yanking on her arm. "Get up, Jenny, for heaven's sake, and give the man your name. You sly devil, you," she bubbled on, oblivious of Jenny's bewildered dismay. "Keep him in the past, indeed. I love it."

Somehow Jenny stood. Had she really bid three hundred dollars for an evening with a man whose company she'd never been able to tolerate for more than three seconds without coming apart at the seams?

"Your name, madam."

"Eugenie Jones."

"Would you please come up here, Ms. Jones."

Jenny began to helplessly shake her head, but Georgette was already pulling away her chair and pushing her forward. "Go on," she urged impatiently. "What's the matter with you?"

David came to meet Jenny by the stairs leading up to the stage. She shot him a hopefully cool glance that he stoically returned as he held out his hand to her.

Jenny gingerly gave him the tips of her icy fingers and snatched them back the instant his hard, warm hand started to swallow them up.

David had nevertheless felt them tremble, and though Jenny's behavior confounded him he felt the need to reassure her.

"It's all right, Stork," he murmured, "I don't bite anymore."

"Well, I do." Head high, Jenny stepped past him toward the beaming emcee.

Bemused, David followed, then stood beside her, taking care not to touch her again.

"Ladies," the master of ceremonies called out, "let's all be good sports and give a round of applause for Ms. Jones and Mr. Waterman. As you are aware, the bachelors have agreed to match dollar for dollar the amount of their lady's bid, and so, thanks to this fine couple, the Homeless Children Fund is six hundred dollars richer."

He turned to Jenny. "If you'd please shake Mr. Waterman's hand, Ms. Jones, for the cameras..."

Blinking against the sudden glare of camera flashlights, Jenny forced herself to turn toward David and smile. Her eyes met his, and just as before, once connected, their gazes seemed to fuse. Something sizzled and arced between them, no doubt the old antagonism multiplied a thousandfold by the passage of time. Whatever, the force of it had Jenny turning and bolting off the stage.

She barely stopped at the table to collect her handbag before she was out of the room and rushing across the hotel lobby to the women's lounge.

Once inside, she sagged against the door. A long, shaky breath escaped her like air from a leaky tire, deflating her just as effectively. She felt as limp as an empty inner tube.

What on earth had possessed her? she wondered crazily. To bid three hundred of her hard-earned dollars on, of all people, *David Waterman!!*

Catching sight of herself in the wall of ornate mirrors across the lounge, she slowly moved toward them. Sinking down onto one of the plush little benches in front of them, she leaned toward her flushed, almost feverish looking image.

"What are you, nuts or something?"

Unless her voice had suddenly changed from alto to bass baritone, Jenny knew she wasn't the one asking that question. She shot to her feet and spun around to face the door.

David Waterman was standing in it, one shoulder propped against the frame, the other holding the door open. His arms and legs negligently crossed, he looked for all the world as if he owned the place.

"Get out of here," Jenny exclaimed in a furious whisper. "Don't you have any sense of propriety? This is the ladies' room, for crying out loud."

"I don't see any ladies, do you?" Brows arched, David made a show of scanning the premises.

"Oh!" Words failed Jenny, as they'd all too often had a way of doing around this maddening individual. "What do you want from me?"

"Funny, that's what I came to ask you."

"Go away."

"Not until you tell me what this is all about." She's gorgeous, David realized with amazement as he watched Jenny's fists ball in helpless frustration and her pansy eyes spout blue flames. His practiced glance took in her willowy length and slim, endless legs, the narrow waist above which surprisingly generous breasts now attracted his gaze like twin magnets.

Unexpected desire flashed like white-hot lightning through his gut. Good *lord,* he thought, had his hormones gone completely out of whack somewhere? Shaken, he forced his eyes back up to hers.

Jenny forbade herself to betray by as much as the flicker of a lash the jolt of reaction David's blatant perusal of her physical attributes had caused. Though she trembled beneath the heat of his silver-green gaze as if he'd reached out a hand and caressed her, she set her jaw and willed frost into her expression. That's all she needed, she told herself, for this jaded Lothario to think her as ripe for the plucking as all the other females he'd sampled and discarded over the years.

The derision David saw in Jenny's eyes was like a dash of icy water. He blinked, effectively putting an end to their emotion-charged standoff. "All right, Stork, why the bid?"

If only she knew! Pretending nonchalance, Jenny shrugged. "Temporary insanity."

"Now that I can believe."

Jenny refused to be charmed by his crooked grin as he added, "I always did say all that reading would turn on you one day. Mental overload."

"Beats a mental vacuum." Habits, it seemed, merely lay dormant, they didn't die. Jenny had fired the shot without even thinking. Seeing his deep flush, however, the expected surge of satisfaction didn't materialize. "I'm sorry—"

"Hey." David pushed away from the doorjamb, his hands palms up. "It's okay. It's how we are, you and I, isn't it? Push and shove, feint and parry, until—pow, one of us draws blood. Remember?"

"Yes."

Though she managed to keep her voice steady, Jenny had to battle an urge to back away as David took a step toward her. Behind him, the lounge door sighed shut.

"So," he said, "do you want to withdraw the bid?"

Jenny couldn't decipher his expression as he asked the question. His tone too was neutral. Still, his nearness was somehow threatening, it made her want nothing so much as to shout, "Yes, I do" and make a run for it.

"No," she said, lifting her chin. "I wouldn't dream of it."

"You realize your so-called prize is an evening on the town with me?"

"Heart be still," Jenny quipped with more bravado than she felt. David wore a cologne that was as seductive as it was subtle. Suddenly breathless, Jenny sucked in some air. The audible tremor of the inhalation made her wish she'd just quietly suffocated instead.

"There'll be dinner, dancing, that kind of stuff," David said. "We'll be expected to look like we're enjoying each other's company." He advanced another step, his eyes narrowing just a little as they snared her gaze. "Do I make you nervous, Storky?"

"Don't call me that."

His brows snapped upward. His grin insolent, he cocked his head to the side and looked her up and down. "You're right," he conceded at length, very softly. "The name no longer fits."

Jenny didn't know what to say, doubted she could have forced a single syllable past the brick stuck sideways in her throat as she reached out and touched her cheek.

"You're looking great, Jen."

The door flew open.

David dropped his hand.

A group of women noisily burst into the room only to fall silent and freeze, arrested by the sight of a male in this strictly female sanctuary.

David gave them all a dazzling smile and moved past them to the door. He gallantly held it while another group entered, then looked back at Jenny with a wink and said, "We've got to stop meeting like this."

With that he was gone, leaving Jenny to explain the situation to the fascinated audience, had she chosen to do so, which she didn't. She left the women to their speculations and went to find the auction desk. There she plunked down a check for three hundred dollars, collared a waiter to give him a message for Georgette and then fled the scene.

Jenny had not slept well.

In the course of her restless tossing, she'd tried again and again to discover what might have motivated her to call out that ridiculous final bid. Unfortunately, temporary insanity had still been the only explanation she'd been able to come up with.

So she awoke grumpy. Her customary four-mile run elevated her mood somewhat, but the picture on the front page of the paper she picked up off her stoop on the way back in, made it plummet clear down to sub-basement again.

Horrified by what her eyes beheld, she stood panting as she stared holes into the photo of David Waterman and herself up on the auction stage. He was looking devastatingly macho and disgustingly pleased with himself, while she...

Jenny groaned. Why, she looked like some witless teenybopper drooling over her favorite rock star!

Jenny knew how she'd *really* felt at the time, of course—intensely annoyed with herself and her big mouth—so it had to be thanks to a distortion of the camera lens that in this photo her expression seemed to convey longing bordering on outright hunger.

She slammed down the paper and wearily leaned her forehead against the cool wood of her front door. This was awful. People would think—

"Why, Jenny Jones, I swear you're in love with the man!"

That's what people would think, and an hour later those were Georgette's exact words. Jenny, hoping to avoid her friend's comments and/or questions for as long as possible, had refused to even acknowledge Georgette's signal, two long buzzes followed by one short. Whereupon Georgette, undaunted, had simply gone to fetch the emergency key Jenny had left with her and let herself in.

She stated her opinion with supreme satisfaction, adding, "And the fact that you're hiding from me confirms it." She gazed lovingly at the picture a moment, then looked sharply back at Jenny. "All right, how long?"

"How long what?" Jenny stepped into her jeans, her motions jerky with impatience as she zipped them.

"How long has this been going on, and don't you dare say it hasn't."

"All right." Because her reply was muffled by the yellow cotton sweater she was pulling over her head, Jenny repeated it more emphatically when she emerged. "All right, I won't."

With pretended calm, she folded back the ribbing at the end of each sleeve and tucked up the sweater's waistband just so.

Georgette watched her narrowly. "What are you saying?"

"Nothing." Jenny stepped up to the mirror, licked the tip of one finger and meticulously smoothed each of her eyebrows. Out of the corner of her eye she could see Georgette begin to fume and took perverse satisfaction in it. "Since there is nothing to say."

"Meaning?"

"Meaning—" Jenny chose white deck shoes from the neat lineup in her closet and stepped into them "—nothing is or has been going on, Georgette." She picked her shoulder bag up off the bed and walked out of the bedroom. "Meaning I do not love the man," she said over one shoulder as she headed for the front door. "I never have and—you can take this to the bank, Georgette—I never will."

When by Wednesday no bellow of outrage from Jenny had come his way as a result of that newspaper picture, David let go a figuratively held breath. Several clients and all of his staff had asked about the new lady in his life, because it was surely obvious from that photo that they were crazy about each other.

Which just went to show what he'd always maintained: People were ever willing to make judgments and form opinions based on nothing more than what they thought they saw.

On his back beneath the vintage Corvette he had restored to gleaming perfection over the past several years, David tightened a nut on the oil pan and grimaced. If that picture had been snapped even one second sooner or later, the impression would more than likely have been one of mutual dislike and they'd all have had a field day with that.

'Course they would've come a lot closer to the truth with that call, he conceded wryly, and followed that concession with a vicious oath as the wrench slipped and he skinned his knuckles.

The portable phone by his feet whirred. Muttering, David scooted out from under the car, sat up too soon and resoundingly conked his head, which elicited enough curses to turn the air blue as he plopped back down onto the ground.

Sucking on the injured knuckles of one hand, he scooted forward a bit further and reached for the phone with his other hand.

"Hello!"

Silence, followed by a hesitant female voice. "Uh, David?"

David snapped upright. "Stor—I mean, *Jenny!*" An unexpected surge of pleasure made him forget his throbbing head, but then he thought, Uh-oh, here it comes about the picture, and the pounding resumed with a vengeance. "How are you?" he added cautiously.

"Fine, thank you." No more hesitation; she sounded her brisk and businesslike self. "And you?"

"Pretty good, considering I just dented my head." David gingerly touched what felt like a sizable goose egg. "You any good at first aid?"

"No."

Frostbite, David thought sourly, just what he needed on top of everything else. "So, uh, what can I do for you?"

"It's about our date. From the auction," Jenny added quickly.

"Yes?" David braced himself for rejection and didn't like one bit the crashing disappointment he felt.

"The committee called me with the particulars, and I— if you have a moment, I thought I'd go over them with you. If you have time."

She's nervous, David realized, catching a breathy quality in Jenny's voice. Now that he knew she wasn't planning to bow out of anything, he could relax and listen to more than just her words. Definitely nervous.

He smiled, ridiculously pleased. "All the time in the world."

"All right. It's a week from Saturday. They'll be sending a limousine and a photographer. I don't know if they'll be together, or what, but shall I tell them to pick me up first? Or you?"

"Me." He stretched out on his back, one foot propped across a knee, his head cushioned on one hand. Admiring the pale blue of the late afternoon sky, he added, "You may not know this, but I am a gentleman, and it is a gentleman's duty to pick his date up, not the other way around."

"Since I can hardly be considered your date, David," Jenny replied repressively, "I'd say the point is moot. As for you being a gentleman—"

"Ye-e-e-s?"

There followed a small pause during which David could all but see Jenny's chin come up.

"Nothing."

"So I'll pick you up then?"

"Fine."

David could have sworn that clipped response had icicles forming inside his ear.

"Dinner will be at Chez Francois," Jenny added stiffly at length, "followed by dancing at the Latin Club."

"Whooppee!"

"There's no need to be snide."

"There is when you make the agenda sound as exciting as a visit to the morgue."

"It's not going to work, is it?"

"Not if you don't lighten up, Storky."

"I asked you not to—"

"Call you that," David finished. "Sorry." He rubbed the back of his neck with a grimace. "Do you have to be so damn prissy, though, Jen? I mean, this is *me* you're talking to. We've known each other for years, for crying out loud. Relax, will you?"

A heavy sigh. "I don't know if I can. With you."

"Could you at least try?" David growled. Because he wanted to reach through the wire and strangle her skinny little neck, he paused to draw breath and moderate his tone. "Look, none of this was my idea, you know...."

"I know. And I'm sorry."

"I don't want you sorry, dammit!" He was on his feet. "I just want you friendly. We're supposed to be having a good time on that *date!*" He spat the word. "Think you can manage that?"

"I can manage anything you can, thank you."

"Terrific!" David slammed the phone against his thigh and counted to ten before lifting it to his ear again. "So what time do the good times start to roll, Ms. Jones?"

"If you insist on being sarcastic..."

"So help me, Jenny—"

"Seven o'clock."

"Great."

Silence. David paced, muttering and wondering why he didn't just tell her to forget it. To find herself another patsy if she could, because he didn't need this sh—

"D-David?"

At the hesitant softness of Jenny's voice, David's head came up. "Yes?"

"I really would like to, you know—" she stopped to clear her throat "—make an effort to get along. I mean, you're right. We're adults, it's for a good cause, and we're supposed to seem as if we're *glad* to be doing this thing...."

"Jenny." With a sigh, David tipped his head back and stared up at the sky. How was it Jenny Jones could still make him feel more tenderness than he'd ever felt for anyone else, yet at the drop of a hat make him want to murder her, too? "Up until you called today, I'd gotten so I *was* kind of glad to be doing this thing."

"You had?" she asked, and after a moment quietly added, "Why?"

"Beats the hell out of me." David shook his head with a mirthless chuckle. "As you know better than anyone, I never was very bright. Or maybe I'm just a glutton for punishment. I don't know—what do you think?"

Chapter Three

Jenny thought her life had certainly been a lot less complicated before David Waterman had strutted back into it. On those rare occasions when she'd thought of him at all over the years, it had been with either indifference or aversion. There had been no ambivalence, none of the push-pull feelings that were confounding her these days.

She could remember having had bouts of similar ambivalence toward him in the course of their youth, however, and that she hadn't liked it then any better than she did now.

By the time the night of their date rolled around, she just wanted the evening to be over with so that she could get on with her life again. Alone.

Getting ready for the date was a trial. It wasn't that Jenny wanted to impress David in any way, of course she didn't. But she was a businesswoman, out on a much publicized date for a good cause. Naturally she wanted to look just right. She changed her clothes three times, took her hair down and put it up again twice and, in the end, left it to tumble in a more or less orderly fashion to her shoulders and past.

Eyeing herself critically in the mirror, she would have done another wardrobe change, but it was nearly seven o'clock, so she forced herself to keep on the pencil-slim black velvet dress. It looked all right, she supposed. Conservative. Its antique white lace collar covered most of her shoulders and chest. Its skirt flared bell-like from the hips and swirled to midcalf. The length flattered her ankles and feet, shod in low-heeled black shoes. The sleeves of the dress were long and fitted, making a wrap unnecessary.

Taking another critical look at herself, Jenny decided the overall effect was one of simple but expensive elegance.

A class act, yet sexy as sin, was how David, well pleased, put it to himself when Jenny stood framed in her doorway after he'd rung the bell.

He handed her a single pink carnation and, feeling again that odd, reluctant stab of tenderness, watched the color in her cheeks heighten to match the flower's vivid hue. She held it to her nose, inhaled its delicate fragrance. "Thank you."

David was charmed by her almost shy smile. "It's not part of the prize," he said, because it seemed somehow important she know that.

"It's lovely." Jenny sniffed at the flower again. "Thank you very much." She stepped aside. "Won't you come in while I put it in water? It seems a shame to carry it with me and let it wilt," she added over her shoulder as she walked away.

David stepped into the tiny living room and looked around. The place was immaculate to the point of sterility; even the throw pillows on the couch seemed starched and at attention. Two magazines lay perfectly aligned with and perpendicular to the edges of the glass-and-chrome coffee table. The plush carpet was cream colored and devoid of either spots or footprints; no knickknacks cluttered the glass end tables. Only a couple of abstracts in thin metal frames relieved the stark whiteness of the walls.

David decided he'd been in hospital rooms cozier than this, and wondered at the woman who'd created this sensual desert. Was it that Jenny had no warmth, no passion? Or was it that she feared she had too much and always worked at keeping it from view?

Recalling the heat with which she used to fight him, he suspected the latter to be the case.

Jenny was back in mere moments. "There," she said, and smiled at him. "I'm ready to go if you are."

"Where'd you put the flower?"

Jenny colored. "In my bedroom. I've got my desk in there." She shrugged. "It's where I spend most of my time when I'm home."

Ah! David nodded to himself. Now there was a room he wouldn't mind seeing. Something told him it would reflect the real Jenny much more accurately than this living room did. Not surprisingly, given the surges of lust she'd been instigating inside him since their recent reunion at the auction, he found himself wanting to know what the real Jenny was like.

"Are you coming?" Jenny was holding the door open with her back and waiting for him to step out into the hall.

David stopped in front of her, looked her in the eye. "You know, you're very beautiful," he said.

Jenny blinked, surprised and disconcertingly pleased by the compliment before conditioned reflexes asserted themselves. "Don't. I know how I look."

David's eyes narrowed. "And how's that?"

Jenny stiffened even more. Only David Waterman would be tactless enough to ask such a thing. "Passably attractive, but hardly beautiful, thank you very much."

David cocked a brow and, catching a lock of her hair, tested its silky softness between thumb and forefinger. He slanted her a look from beneath indecently long lashes. "What's the matter, Stork?" he murmured. "Haven't you heard that beauty is in the eye of the beholder?"

"Yes, I have," Jenny managed to reply. "But what with you being the beholder..." She pointedly let the sentence hang.

"Ouch." Grinning, David covered his heart with his hand. "That hurts."

Jenny's response was an inelegant sort of half snort as she ducked away from him into the hall where she barely stopped herself from fanning her flushed face. It was disgusting, she thought, that throughout their interchange all she'd been able to think of was how good David looked, how delicious he smelled. And to wonder how a man who appeared so outwardly cool could radiate so much animal heat. She'd felt overcome by it, by *him* and his closeness, and she didn't like her reactions one bit.

"This isn't going to work, you know," she said, making a project out of brushing imaginary bits of lint from her sleeve and avoiding his eyes.

"What, again?" David gripped Jenny's elbow and briskly hustled her into the elevator. "And here I've been as charming as can be."

The elevator door swooshed shut behind them. "Well, could you not be, for a change?"

Though she stood staring straight ahead, Jenny could tell from the tone of his voice that David was stifling laughter as he drawled, "I don't know—I've never tried."

The elevator stopped and the door glided open just as Jenny gave in to helpless laughter. The man was impossible.

She was still smiling—and acutely aware of David's gently guiding hand at the small of her back—when they stepped through her building's plate glass double doors. A flash popped brightly, blinding her, and she blinked.

"Nice shot," the bearded man with the camera said as they came abreast of him. His eyes did a rapid up and down inspection of Jenny's velvet-clad person, and he whistled softly through his teeth. "Ooh-la-la! This assignment is beginning to look better and better."

"Meet Brian Fuller, Jenny," David said with a small smile, though the urge to tell the man to keep his eyes and comments to himself was as unexpected as it was strong.

"Mr. Fuller." Jenny's nod was cool. Hers had never been the kind of looks to inspire wolf whistles, and so the reporter's heavy-handed flattery set her teeth on edge. It was bad enough to have to put up with David Waterman's practiced lines for tonight.

Fuller stuck out his hand. "A pleasure, Ms. Jones. And since I'm gonna be your shadow tonight, so to speak, why'nt you call me Brian."

Jenny briefly shook his hand. "How d'you do."

"I'm doin' just fine, thanks, now that you're here. How about one more picture as you help the lady into the limo, Waterman?"

Fuller turned, camera cocked, as David did as he asked. Jenny smiled a greeting at the driver, who stood holding the limousine door for her.

"Yeah," Fuller drawled, "that's it, babe. Nice bit of leg, too. Got it."

Babe. Jenny ground her teeth, yanked down her skirt and settled herself in the roomy comfort of the back seat.

"The man's right about your legs," David murmured, getting in after her. "But if he keeps talking to you like that I just may have to break both of his."

He said it conversationally, but something in his eyes told Jenny he was perfectly willing and capable of doing the deed.

"In a pinch, I'd do it myself," she told him, adding with a glance across his shoulder, "Better stop scowling, I think he's headed toward us again. We wouldn't want him to think we're not enjoying ourselves."

"Heaven forbid." They exchanged tentative smiles that somehow lingered. David said, "And are we?"

A shiver tickled along Jenny's spine. Maybe she should have brought a coat, after all, she thought, but knew it wasn't from cold that her skin puckered.

"I am," she said, a little breathlessly. "Trying to, in any case."

The air between seemed to sizzle as the moment lengthened. David sucked in a sharp breath, and Jenny felt as if in doing so he'd stolen hers. She watched his eyes darken and his gaze flick to her lips, and her mouth went dry. Her lips parted.

"Yo, Waterman." Fuller stuck his head through the open window, and David jerked back with a muffled oath. "I'll catch you guys later at Chez Francois." He leered at Jenny, then winked at David. "Enjoy."

"I'd like to punch that man right in the nose," Jenny snapped as soon as David had rolled up the window.

"I think that's supposed to be my line," he said.

"Not in this century."

That made him laugh, and the awareness humming between them eased. "How could I forget, you're a nineties woman," he quipped.

"And proud of it."

In the silence that followed, the car left her building's parking lot, and David turned to stare out of his window. Glad to have a moment's respite, Jenny too looked out at the street. Realizing how tense she'd been moments before, she forced herself to relax. In retrospect, she was grateful for Fuller's interruption, aware it had forestalled her doing something foolish. She was sure David had been thinking about kissing her just then, and she would have let him if he'd tried. She had to be crazy!

David was reaching similar conclusions about his particular mental state. He was assessing the increasingly potent reactions Jenny Jones was arousing in him. Just by being near. Or by looking at him. Her scent, something crisp and elusive like herself, beckoned to him. The fathomless depths of her pansy eyes seemed to urge him to plunge in. Her lips seemed shaped for his kiss.

He wanted her, and, considering she made no bones about wanting him as much as she wanted a dose of the flu, he inwardly winced. He *had* to be really stupid to be sitting here hankering.

He turned to glance at her and, seeing her face partially averted, took advantage of that fact to leisurely study her profile. As always, he was struck by how classy her exquisite bone structure made her look. Snooty, he used to think she was. A snob, and, of course, there'd never been anything in her behavior toward him to make him believe Russell's protestations that she was nothing of the kind.

She'd eyeball him down that arrogant little nose of hers and, because she made him feel every bit the ignorant jock that he'd been, and because just once he wanted her to look at him the way other girls did, he'd make some crack about her bean-pole shape or big ears—going for a laugh from his adoring fans at Jenny's expense. Whereupon she'd turn red as a cranberry and furiously slash him to ribbons with that whip of a tongue of hers.

Things hadn't changed much, he thought wryly. Storky Jones could still make him feel ignorant, and he still wanted her to look at him the way many other women did: seductively, covetously. She still didn't, but he no longer found her body anything to joke about. As to her ears . . .

Impulsively he reached out and with one finger gently swept a swirl of hair out of the way.

Startled, Jenny's head swung toward him, making his finger graze her cheek. It felt as velvety as her dress. "What?"

"I just realized your ears are different."

Jenny blushed. Scarlet. It infuriated her and enchanted him. "I, uh..." She tried for an offhand shrug. "I've had them, you know . . . fixed."

"Fixed?" He traced the delicate shell. "Were they broken?"

He was making fun of her. Jenny bristled and felt much better. She had plenty of defenses against David Waterman's teasing; what she found she couldn't handle was the unsettlingly seductive side he seemed determined to show her tonight.

"You know very well what they were."

"Pitcher handles?" David found he couldn't resist, she looked so damn beautiful when she got riled.

"Why, you—"

His finger moved to cover her mouth and cut off whatever verbal volley she'd been about to fire at him. "Truce, remember?"

Blue flames flickered in her narrowed eyes and heated David's blood. Oh yes, he thought, there's passion here, all right.

Before good sense and second thoughts could interfere, he leaned over and gently caught her earlobe between his teeth. Very gently, he bit it, then softly kissed the spot and withdrew. He knew if he didn't, he'd be all over her in just another second.

The cocky grin he tossed her as she stared at him in shock took considerable effort.

Jenny had no idea how come she was still sitting upright when every bone in her body had just been liquefied. Because her hands were shaking, she tightly folded them in her lap, even though she wanted desperately to reach up and touch the spot where David's mouth had been. It burned, that spot, tingled and prickled ...

Like a case of poison ivy.

Where that thought had come from, Jenny had no idea, but she welcomed it with open arms. It made her smile and brought what just happened into perspective before her fevered imagination could blow it way out of proportion. Her hands relaxed, the starch returned to her bones.

"You're crazy," she told him, proud of her steady voice and level tone. "You know that, don't you?"

David nodded. *About you, I'm beginning to think.* "So I've been told. It has its moments, you know. You ought to give it a shot."

"I already did."

"Oh? When?"

"The night I bid on you at that auction."

An elevator took them up to Chez Francois on the fifty-second floor of the Civic Bank Building. A bowing maître d' ushered them to a white-clothed table along one of the walls of windows.

Jenny took in the view of Seattle harbor, Elliott Bay and Alki Point across the water as she was being seated. Everywhere lights cast long and sparkling reflections, gilding the daytime ordinariness of the waterfront and transforming it the way a lighted Christmas tree transforms even the most dreary of rooms. One of the commuter ferries, a blaze of lights bestowing on it all the glamor of a luxury cruise ship, detached itself from shore and majestically plowed across the bay. Its foaming wake shone iridescent white.

"I really love this city." Jenny's eyes, shifting to David across the table from her, shone. "Maybe it's because it's my hometown, but I think it's the most beautiful place in the world."

"And still you stayed away from it for ten years." He said it softly, yet Jenny thought she detected a hint of accusation.

She bit her lip. "Yes, I did."

"You didn't even come back for vacations."

"No, I didn't."

"And why was that?"

Jenny tugged her napkin out of its fancy arrangement in the water glass. "If you'll remember, my parents had moved to Florida...."

"The Daltons were still here." And with that statement Russell Dalton's ghost joined them at their table. "They needed you, Jenny."

"And I was there for them. Even after I moved to Washington, we talked on the phone all the time. Besides—" Dropping the napkin she'd been toying with into her lap, Jenny looked him in the eye. "They still had you."

"Yeah." He said it bitterly, and for several heartbeats neither spoke. "Tell me, Jen," David finally said, "do you still blame me for what happened?"

Jenny had expected the question to come up. She supposed they might as well get it out of the way. "No."

"Can you look at me and say that?"

Slowly Jenny raised her gaze to David's. His expression was neutral, but she'd been around him long enough now to see the tension and vulnerability the careful blankness was supposed to conceal.

Moved, and compelled by an almost painful urge to comfort and reassure him, she impulsively reached across the table and laid her palm against his cheek. "No, David," she said softly. "It wasn't your fault."

She felt his jaw unclench beneath her touch. Covering her hand with his, he turned his face and pressed his lips against her palm. "Thank you."

"Don't." As if burned, Jenny snatched back her hand. The intimacy of that kiss completely unnerved her. "This really isn't going to work," she said shakily, "if you keep doing stuff like that."

"What isn't?" he asked, and the husky timbre of his voice excited her, too.

"The truce we declared for tonight."

"Ah, yes, the truce." Something flickered in his eyes before he added, "Do we really need one between us, Jen? Are we still at war then, you and I?"

Jenny's eyes were about to get caught up in his searching ones, and she quickly averted them. "I don't know."

"Why'd you bid on me at the auction, Jenny, if we're still fighting?"

"I don't know that, either." Jenny's little frown reflected genuine bewilderment. "I'm still trying to figure that one out myself."

"When you've got it figured," Dave said, "will you tell me?"

"All right."

"Scout's honor?"

"You were never a Scout." Even to herself the intended dig sounded feeble, but the intensity of David's regard was doing terrible things to Jenny's emotional equilibrium. "You were more into going and leading astray."

David's grin showed no regrets. "Speaking of which," he said, "how about we have some champagne?" At Jenny's weak nod, he raised a hand. "Waiter..."

Jenny was glad for the breather David's subsequent consultation with the sommelier afforded her. She felt slightly shell-shocked from the relentless assaults David seemed intent on launching on her senses and emotions, and from her own, not very successful, defensive maneuvers. They might not be waging war the way they used to, she reflected, but some sort of battle was still going on. Could it be that, given their history, ordinary conversation simply wasn't possible between them? If so, it was going to be a long evening.

"So tell me what you've been doing with yourself all these years," she said, as soon as the waiter had gone.

"Me?" David shrugged. "Flying, mostly."

"You still love it, then."

"Yep. I guess I'm a stick-to-one-thing kind of guy."

Except when it comes to women, I'll bet. Angry with herself for that thought, Jenny took a sip of water to wash down the bitter taste it had put in her mouth.

"How about you?" David asked. "Hobnobbing with foreign diplomats and such in D.C., I guess, huh?"

"More than I care to remember." Jenny forced her mind to order. "When I first got to Washington, I thought, wow, this'll be so neat. Parties, receptions, all the best people..." Remembering her naïveté, she laughed. "Let me tell you something, pal—those so-called best people are the biggest collection of snobs you'd ever want to meet. With a few exceptions, of course."

"Like that attaché from San Mariela, for instance?"

"What?" Startled by David's softly voiced question, Jenny blushed.

"Ramirez, wasn't it? Juan?"

"Jose." She told herself it was totally asinine to be feeling guilty. "He was a good friend, yes." Her chin lifted. "How did you know about him?"

"Bea and Frank, who else?" David smiled, while inwardly trying to convince himself it was hunger, not retroactive jealousy, twisting his gut. "I see them from time to time, though not as often as I'd like. They showed me some pictures you'd sent. You were on vacation at the man's hacienda, or something."

"Yes." That had been three years ago, and Jose had proposed to her on that vacation. Only very briefly had Jenny been tempted to accept, and then more out of the romance of the moment than anything else. She'd liked Jose immensely, but...

"Separate bedrooms?"

"What?" Jenny gaped at David, stunned.

"Sorry." David lifted both hands, palms up. "I was way off base with that one."

"I'll say." Jenny glared at him.

"Hey, I said I was sorry." Neither spoke for a moment, and both of them looked everywhere but at each other. After a while, David, his gaze on the water glass he was pushing around, said softly, "Kind of old for you, wasn't he?"

"Excuse me?" Jenny sat stiffly erect. How dare he? she fumed. Just where did he get off to question her like this? And, anyway, Jose hadn't been old, he'd been mature. A wonderful man, full of the kinds of good qualities that were glaringly lacking in David Waterman's character.

"Why didn't you marry him? Or didn't he ask you?"

"As a matter of fact, he did." Why was she even dignifying his odious questions with a reply? Jenny wondered furiously.

To her everlasting relief, the champagne arrived. When it was poured, and they were once again alone, an increasingly pregnant pause followed. Jenny fussed with the cuffs of her dress and smoothed her napkin; David cleared his throat a few times.

"If you don't do it too violently," he finally said, "I think you could kick my shin under the table and nobody'd notice."

He looked at her so drolly, Jenny's indignation flew right out the wall of windows. She stared at him a moment, then covered her eyes with one hand and, laughing, helplessly shook her head. "I can't believe any of this is really happening."

"It is kind of weird, being here together, isn't it?" David concurred.

Jenny dropped her hand. "More than weird."

"I'll drink to that." Jenny's soft, answering laugh made David grin. He raised his glass, waited for her to follow suit. "Cheers."

They sipped, eyes on each other, smiles fading.

Jenny concentrated on keeping her hand steady. Why did eye contact with David unnerve her so? She made a project out of setting her glass down on the table and suddenly wished Fuller, the photographer, were there—anything—to forestall these bouts of awareness and tension between David and herself.

Shifting in her seat, she cast around for a topic with which to end this latest charged silence.

"Waterman Aviation," she finally mused. "By the sound of that you're a businessman as well as a flyer."

David, too, shifted in his chair. He stuck a finger in his collar and stretched his chin as if things had gotten too tight for him somehow. "'Fraid so."

"You don't like it?"

He shrugged. "Flying is all I ever really wanted to do, but since I like to be my own boss, too, that meant I had to go into business for myself. Now the running of that business takes up the bulk of my time."

"You could've taken a partner," Jenny pointed out. "You know, where you do all the flying, he does all the book work. Something like that."

"Believe me, I've thought about it."

Picking up his glass, David leaned back with it but didn't drink. Instead he thoughtfully studied its effervescent contents. "The thing is," he went on, "a partnership tends to be like a marriage—you'd better be damn sure you know what you're letting yourself in for, and who you're doing it with."

He drank deeply and, setting down the glass, looked Jenny straight in the eye as he added, "So far I haven't met anyone I'd like to be partners with."

The temptation to ask if he'd met anyone he'd like to be married to was strong, but Jenny resisted. With more difficulty than she liked, but nevertheless, she did resist.

"I know what you mean," she murmured into her glass, and took another sip before setting it down. "Bill Shafer offered to become a silent partner in my business. God knows, accepting his offer would have made this first year a lot easier, but I, too, like my independence. Life's simpler that way."

"Lonelier too, though, don't you find?"

Apparently David saw no need to resist the temptation to probe into her personal life once again, Jenny thought. "I'm not lonely."

"Ever?"

"Not often enough to change the status quo."

"The status quo being, quote, contented to be single, unquote?"

"You saw the show," Jenny exclaimed. *Timely Topics.*"

David grinned. "Guilty. It's how I knew you were back in town."

"You knew." Jenny frowned at him. "Yet you didn't call...."

"Should I have?"

"I guess not."

"I wanted to, you know."

"Are you ready to order, sir?" Unnoticed, the waiter had materialized at their table. "Perhaps an appetizer? I can recommend the Dungeness Crab Cocktail."

"Jenny?" David deferred. "Are you ready for something?"

"Yes." Jenny pounced on the diversion. "Yes, I am. Starved, in fact."

"You heard the lady." David turned to her again. "The crab cocktail sound good?"

"Wonderful."

"Why don't you bring us two of those then and leave the menus," David instructed the waiter. "We'll order the rest when you bring the appetizer."

"Very good, sir."

The waiter refilled their glasses, then disappeared.

"So what all does Waterman Aviation entail?" Jenny asked quickly, anxious to fill the momentary silence before David had a chance to speak. "Just charters, or...?"

"We're an FBO." The slowness of his reply told Jenny her tactic had been noted. "A Fixed Base Operation. You know, like Russ and I worked for through college. We do maintenance, some selling, flight school, charter, gas, tie-ups, you name it.''

"You *are* busy.''

Her observation made him laugh. "I may not have a partner, but I do have help, you know." He shook his head at her, chuckling. "Besides me, there's a senior pilot and a couple of instructors for the flight school, a couple of mechanics, a secretary, receptionist, the works. Quite a nice operation, if I do say so myself. You ought to come by and see it sometime. I'll even take you up for a spin...."

"I'm not very fond of planes."

"Still?"

"Nothing's happened to make me feel better about them."

There was Russell's ghost again. "I s'pose not."

"Why don't we see what's good to eat," Jenny said brightly, cutting into the lengthening silence. "I really am hungry."

They read the menu, made their choices and were about midway through their meal when Brian Fuller sauntered in.

"Still eating?" Uninvited he snagged a chair from a nearby table and joined them. "Looks good," he said, helping himself to a hard roll. "Mind if I borrow your knife and some butter, Waterman? I had another job to take care of and haven't had a bite since lunch."

David mutely pushed his bread plate and knife closer to the reporter. "Want me to order you something?"

"Uh-uh." Fuller chewed. "No time. Gotta get a picture of the two of you here, then hustle you over to the Latin Club, take another picture and split. Night court. Not the TV show," he added as an aside to Jenny, "the real thing. Gotta cover it."

Jenny had figured that out for herself but smiled politely. "Sounds interesting."

"It's a drag." He stuffed the rest of the bun into his mouth and got up. "Picture time."

David was a fantastic dancer, and Jenny had always loved to dance. The Latin Club was dimly lit and intimate, the music south of the border, the dance floor packed with undulating bodies.

Brian Fuller had departed long ago.

The rumba rhythms pulsed in Jenny's blood. Pressed against David's length from breast to knee, she was breathtakingly aware of every muscular inch of him. One of his legs brushed the insides of her thigh with every move of the dance they were executing in the minimum of space allotted to them in this crowd.

With one set of their hands clasped and cradled between them, David's other one lay splayed and low on Jenny's back, holding her to him, forcing her pelvis to move against his with every step of the dance.

Jenny's free hand clutched David's shoulder with real need as the sensations, called forth by the intimacy of their positions and movements, were causing her knees to go weak with reaction.

David's gaze was relentlessly locked on hers. His expression mirrored and magnified the cravings the proximity of their bodies and the hot, pulsing beat of the music aroused in Jenny, and increased the feeling of weakness in her legs.

Thanks to their near equal height, their faces were so close they breathed each other's breath. Their lips were scant inches apart. And suddenly not at all. Without warning, without releasing Jenny from the smoldering prison of his gaze, David had closed the small gap and joined her to him as fully as was possible under the circumstances.

Electrified, Jenny responded to his kiss with all the hunger that had steadily grown with each dance. Her feet stopped moving. Her lips parted beneath the insistent pressure of his to admit his tongue and to meet it with her own slick and searching one. His groan, deep and elemental, reverberated in her mouth, and when the pressure of his hand on her back increased and moved lower, she accommodated him by rising on tiptoe and fitting herself more completely against him.

And all the while they swayed to the primitive rhythm of the music. A part of it. Filled with it.

And then it stopped.

Applause.

Jenny and David jerked apart, disoriented, throbbing with unfulfilled desires. Jenny blinked until her vision cleared enough to take in her surroundings. Another splash of heat, unrelated to passion, stained her cheeks as her gaze flew to David. He was still holding her hand, and he was watching her with an unreadable expression.

She dredged up a small laugh from somewhere and touched her forehead. "Phew. Hot in here..."

He squeezed her hand. "Jenny, listen..."

"No, no." She laughed again—rather pitifully, she had to admit—and pulled her hand from his. "Don't."

She turned and led the way to their little table, glad that her back was to him and she no longer had to see the look of apology in his eyes. That's all she needed just then, to have him say he was sorry about what had happened. If anyone should be sorry it was she, but try as she might she couldn't detect one iota of regret in the turbulent mishmash of her emotions just then. Later, when she was completely sane again, she probably would, but for the moment it was all she could do to come to grips with what

had happened out there. The kind of passion she'd felt . . .
Frankly she'd never have thought she had it in her.

"Jenny."

They were at their table, and Jenny had little choice but
to turn around and face him. "Yes?"

"I think we should talk about this."

She shook her head, firming her jaw and pressing her
lips together to keep her chin from wobbling. Unbidden,
tears burned the back of her eyes. She blindly groped for
her chair, gripped it, then sank down onto it.

"Let's go home, Jen."

Home. Of course. There was no way they could stay,
make small talk or dance again after what had just occurred between them. Jenny knew that. Lord knows, she
wouldn't be able to handle a repeat, didn't want to have to,
in any case. But she hated for the night to end, too.

She picked up her small purse and rose.

David stood aside, then trailed her out of the club. They
stood in silence on the sidewalk while the doorman hailed
the waiting limousine.

Once inside, they sat in their respective corners without
touching or speaking. They each stared out the window,
seeing little, registering less.

David's thoughts and feelings were every bit as much in
chaos as Jenny's were. He'd been around the block enough
times with enough women to know that the things he'd felt
while kissing Jenny meant he was in deep trouble here.
Trouble like he'd never been in before. The kind of trouble that could cause a man to make a major mistake, if he
wasn't careful.

He'd known for a long time that he wanted Jenny Jones,
had known it almost as long as he'd known her, as a matter of fact. Part of it had been the challenge of tumbling
her off that snooty perch of hers, to somehow prove him-

self to her the only way he'd known how—with physicality. But another, bigger and better, part had had to do with *feelings*. There'd always been something endearingly awkward about her, a coltishness that had tugged at his heartstrings much as bumbling kittens or puppies did. Like that baby deer, Jenny had been all limbs and hadn't known quite how to maneuver them.

Well, she knew how to maneuver them now!

Sweat popped out all over him as he recalled how she'd felt in his arms, pressed against him, moving against him. He was six foot two, and she was the tallest woman he'd ever danced with. So now he knew what he'd been missing! There was a lot to be said for having every strategic body part perfectly aligned with your own....

He heaved a sigh. All of that didn't help him figure out where, if anywhere, he wanted to go from here. With anyone else the answer would be easy: to bed, posthaste, and via the shortest possible route. But this wasn't just anybody else, this was Storky Jones. His best friend's girl, his best friend's fiancée. His *dead* best friend's fiancée.

He wondered what Russell would want for them.

Can't you guys be friends?

David turned toward Jenny and caught her staring at him. Wide-eyed, alarmed. Puzzled.

"What?" he said softly.

She looked away with a quick shake of the head, then abruptly faced him again. "David, what do you want from me?"

He could remind her that *she* was the one who'd instigated this entire chain of events by bidding on him at the auction that night, and that he might well ask what it was she wanted from *him*. But he didn't. Not because he didn't want to know—he did, very much—but because he was convinced she didn't know the answer to that question any more than he did.

"Friendship?"

"That's all?" Why wasn't she relieved? Jenny wondered wildly. Why this deflating sense of...disappointment?

"Yes, that's all." David picked up her hand, raised it, pressed his lips against the knuckles. His eyes never leaving hers, he added, "At least for now."

Chapter Four

Jenny and Russell were fighting. Before David Waterman had strutted into their lives four years ago, disagreements between them had been pretty rare. Now they were all too frequent and fell into three categories: about David, because of David, instigated by David.

The fight they were having today was all three.

They were juniors at the University of Washington. By some unlucky chance, as far as Jenny was concerned, a class of David's had been canceled. Shop 301, no doubt, she'd remarked snidely to Russell, hoping for a laugh, but instead of laughing Russ had promptly invited David to join them for lunch at Drumheller Fountain.

The fountain was a beautiful spot for a picnic lunch: lush, sloping lawns, an abundance of flowers surrounding it; Lake Washington, just a long stone's throw away. On a clear day the view of Mount Rainier from there was breathtaking. It was one of Jenny's favorite spots on campus.

Except now David Waterman's obnoxious presence spoiled it.

Worse, he hadn't brought a lunch of his own and was mooching the one she'd prepared for Russell and herself.

"Great sandwich, Stork," he said around a mouthful of egg salad. And just when she thought maybe she should stop looking for faults and give him a chance, he added, "If you like salty upchuck on white cardboard, that is."

She wanted to kill him then.

And Russ, no doubt catching the feral gleam in her eye, smiled at her and said, "Now, Jen. You know David's just kidding."

Sure.

Deciding it was best to ignore David Waterman, Jenny took another bite of apple and turned so that her back was to him.

"I checked the paper," she said to Russ, "and the movie starts at 7:10. Which means—"

"Oh, damn!" Russell looked thunderstruck. "Is that tonight?"

"Well, yes..."

"Then I can't go."

"What?"

"He said," David drawled from behind her, "he can't—"

Jenny whipped around to silence him with a cutting glance. "I heard what he said."

"Then why did you say 'what'?"

"It was an exclamation of disbelief, you space cadet." She crossed her arms tightly across her chest and glared at him. "I suppose I have you to thank for this."

"Me?" Dave widened his eyes in mock innocence, took the apple out of her hand and calmly commenced to eat it.

With a garbled sound of furious frustration, Jenny swung around to Russell. "Why can't you go?" she demanded. "And why didn't you say anything yesterday when we talked about this?"

"I thought you meant Tuesday next week." Russell took her hand. "Look, I'm sorry, Jen. It's Mr. Slater. His little nephew is in town. Dave was supposed to take him up for a plane ride, but the kid took a shine to me, instead. I'm stuck, Jen." He smiled coaxingly. "You can come, too, if you want."

She merely snorted, which was the answer Russ had obviously expected, given her aversion to airplanes. He beamed. "All right then, why don't you go to the movie with David? It'll give you guys a chance—"

Jenny's instant and heartfelt, "No, thanks," came simultaneous with David's, "Sure, what's playing?"

"Since it isn't *Rocky*," Jenny drawled contemptuously, "I doubt there's any point in telling you the title, Waterman. People don't beat each other to a pulp in this film, and they use words of more than one syllable, so believe me, you wouldn't be interested."

David's lip curled in a sneer; his eyes turned bright green and hostile. "Oh, yeah?"

Russell sharply said, "Jenny!"

"What?" She defiantly swiveled to face him, all the while trying to ignore the stab of shame she felt.

"Do you always have to be so damn bitchy to David?"

Jenny had no immediate answer, and before she could come up with a fitting rationalization, David spoke from behind her.

"Hey, Russ. Don't sweat it, man, the feeling's mutual. Besides," he drawled, getting to his feet in one fluid motion, "I hate to say this, her being your girlfriend and all, but it'd ruin my reputation, me going out with a nerdy egghead like her.''

''Why, you...'' Hurt propelled Jenny onto her feet as swiftly, if not as gracefully, as he. ''Why don't you grow up!'' she raged, hands balled into fists and ready to sock him.

Russell stepped between them. He looked silently from one to the other, his expression one of bewilderment rather than anger.

''What is it with you two?'' he asked softly. ''Why can't you be friends? You know it'd mean the world to me....''

Friendship between Jenny and David, that's what Russell had wanted. Now David was saying he wanted that, too.

All right. Maybe she owed it to Russell to make the effort, but what was she to make of David's qualifying ''for now''? Friendship would be challenge enough for her without having the specter of Lord knows what complications hanging over her head.

Because her heart was racing, Jenny slowed to a jog near the crest of the hill. She ran five days a week, rain or shine, no matter her whereabouts. It was a great way to stay in shape and at the same time get most of her heavy thinking done. She wasn't too thrilled to find David Waterman monopolizing her thinking time these days. Nothing but trouble, that guy, she groused, breathing hard, even the path to friendship with him seemed full of tricky potholes.

Jenny was running in her old neighborhood tonight, which was still the senior Dalton's home ground. David had lived in the house on one side of the Daltons and she had lived on the other side. Unlike David, however, she had lived next to Russ all of her life; she'd grown up with him. The two of them had shared kindergarten and grade school, visits from the tooth fairy, skinned knees and birthday parties. They'd gone through junior high school together; they'd become inseparable.

Until that summer before their senior year when the Watermans had moved into the neighborhood. Then David and flying had usurped her special spot in Russ's life. Even though Russell insisted that it wasn't so, she'd never been able to forgive David for being Russell's other best friend.

And she'd refused to go flying, period.

Panting, muttering under her breath, Jenny slowed some more. This hill had never used to wind her like this. Why, all through grade school she'd run and bicycled up and down its steep slope without having to draw even one additional breath. Was she getting old or just not concentrating?

A passing car honked its horn. Toot-toot, two short blasts. Jenny raised an arm in greeting without looking up from the ground she was doggedly covering. She knew it was Beatrice Dalton who, along with her husband, taught at the elementary school at the bottom of the hill. She was on her way home now, three blocks away.

She was still in the garage when Jenny trotted up. Her facial expression was wry. "You're a much healthier shade of purple than you were when you ran here a couple of weeks ago," she teased. "I guess that means you're on your way."

"Yes, but to what?" Jenny panted, twisting and stretching and walking in small circles in order to get her heart rate down. "Sometimes I think a coronary."

Bea laughed, and Jenny followed her through a cluttered family room into an equally cluttered kitchen. Housework was not a priority with the Daltons.

"What time will Pop be home?"

"He'll be a little late tonight." Bea dropped her purse and jacket onto the nearest chair. "A staff meeting. I thought we'd eat about six-thirty or seven, if that's all right with you."

"That's fine." Jenny turned on the tap, let the water run over her fingers until it felt cold enough, then filled a glass. Sipping, trying not to gulp it, she leaned a hip against the counter. "Problems?"

"Aren't there always, in one form or another?" Beatrice pulled a plastic-wrapped chicken from the freezer compartment. "Do you think this'll thaw out and cook in two hours? Only three pounds," she mused, then answered herself, "It should."

"Why don't we have a salad, or spaghetti, or something?" Jenny said. "It's just us."

"Oh." Bea turned to her. "Didn't I tell you?" Her expression of innocence had Jenny's eyes narrowing.

"Tell me what?"

"That Davey Waterman called this morning."

Jenny twisted around to carefully put the glass into the sink, then folded her arms across her chest. "No, you didn't."

"Oh." Beatrice busied herself with the chicken. "Well, he did. And you know," she rushed on, "I was so tickled to hear from him after all this time—it's been almost a year, you know—that I insisted he come for dinner."

"I see."

"He was delighted to accept. Especially after I told him you'd be here, too."

"Really."

That dry rejoinder obviously gave Bea pause. Her expression grew more innocent still, to Jenny a clear sign of a guilty conscience. "You don't mind, do you?"

Jenny caught the gleam in the older woman's eye and in her mind saw and heard Yente, the old Anatevka matchmaker. *Do I have a match for you!*

Beatrice had always regarded Jenny as her daughter, and though both she and Frank had loved the idea of Jenny and Russell's marriage, they'd considered that a bonus, nothing more. They would have loved Jenny no less without that additional bond. Which was why, when Russell's death put an end to that dream forever, it had only been a matter of time before Bea had begun to feel compelled to find happiness for Jenny elsewhere.

Ever since she'd come back—unattached, in spite of Bea's hopes for Jose Ramirez—Bea had been trying to "fix Jenny up" with varying degrees of subtlety. Several of the Daltons' younger, single colleagues had thus happened by just before dinner when Jenny was there and been invited to stay; others of their acquaintance had come to Jenny's office on some pretext or other. And then there'd been that Justin Somebody who had quite simply called and announced, "Beatrice tells me you're available...."

It was annoying, but—Jenny stifled a grin—rather funny, too. Especially since she had no plans whatever of getting caught by any of Pop and Bea's schemes.

And so she said, "Why should I mind?" brushing at an imaginary spot on her running shorts and thinking, Two can play this game. "I can put up with David Waterman for one more evening."

"Oh, dear." Bea looked gratifyingly discomfited before she brightened. "You have to give some men a chance, Jen." She tossed the chicken into the microwave and slammed the door. "I assumed from that latest set of newspaper pictures..."

Jenny pushed away from the sink. "You know what they say, Bea. Never assume, because when you assume you make an a—"

"Yes, yes, I know. I *know*." Beatrice impatiently waved Jenny's teasing aside. She switched to Defrost and set the timer. "But your evening out together was a success, wasn't it? I mean, you both looked positively radiant...."

"Hmm." Jenny cut the line on that fishing expedition with a noncommittal shrug, delighting in Bea's look of disappointment. "I guess I'd better run upstairs and shower."

"All right." Bea's smile was grim. "I did tell him to come early so we could all have a good visit."

I'll just bet you did, Jenny thought, gleefully adding, It breaks the heart to disappoint you, old girl, but your efforts are doomed. I might have grown to tolerate David Waterman in the course of our evening together, but that will be—moments of heated palpitations and possible attempts at friendship notwithstanding—as far as things will go. Period.

Humming, Jenny started up the stairs toward the room that had been hers ever since her junior year at college. Her father had taken early retirement for health reasons, and he and her mother had seen no point in postponing their move to Florida when the Daltons were so obviously delighted to have Jenny stay with them.

Jenny had been equally delighted. Here was her chance to be with Russell even more. Living with him under the same roof, she'd reasoned, was bound to bring them close again emotionally. And shut David out. Wrong!

Climbing the stairs, Jenny shook her head, amazed to suddenly realize how much of her thoughts and deeds had revolved around David Waterman in those days. And that had been when she hadn't even liked him!

The notion that followed arrested her steps and soured her mood: Now that she no longer disliked him, would her life revolve around him even more?

The doorbell rang.

"Get that before you go up, will you, dear?" Bea called. "I've got my hands in something."

Still frowning, Jenny made an about-face and went back down the stairs. She opened the door and could only stare when she saw it was David on the other side of it.

The quick once-over he gave her, and the lazy grin that followed, made her heartbeat quicken and her dander rise. She just knew she looked a fright with her face still mottled from sweat and exertion, her hair plastered damply to her head, and likewise her T-shirt and shorts to her body.

He, on the other hand, looked fantastic, dressed casually in a cotton sweater of a bold multihued design and faded jeans that made the most of his lean hips and long legs. The back of his light brown hair touched the top of the tucked-in collar of the yellow cotton shirt he wore under the sweater. His greenish gray eyes, ringed by the kind of lashes any woman would kill for, crinkled endearingly at the corners.

"Bea said casual," he drawled with one more all-enveloping, twinkling glance, "but you're giving the term a whole new meaning."

Thoroughly vexed with him for any number of reasons, not all of them valid, logical or pertinent, Jenny let a narrow-eyed glare convey what she thought of his humor. "It's as rude to be early as it is to be late," she said sententiously.

"So should I come back in half an hour?"

"Don't be ridiculous." She felt like a shrew, especially when in reply to her statement his brows rose with meaningful amusement—as in, *me* ridiculous? Still she tried to be more gracious. "For heaven's sake, come in."

"Why, thank you." He stepped past her into the hall. "Don't mind if I do."

Once inside though he didn't keep going and so, when she had closed the door and turned, they were nose to nose.

The only thing one retreating step accomplished was to bring Jenny's back flush against the door. She stood, breathlessly frozen, sure he meant to kiss her and, for all her furious inward denials, looking forward to it. He moved a little closer. Jenny felt her eyelids begin to flutter and drift. And then, just before her vision blurred and she thought the moment was at hand, one single yellow rosebud appeared in the small space between her face and David's.

"Hi, friend."

The words, spoken in a tone that stroked along her nerve ends like the tender-rough lick of a kitten's tongue, had Jenny's lids pop back up. It took the length of several erratic heartbeats for their gazes to disentangle and for Jenny to find her voice.

"Oh..." was all she managed to say, however.

"It's from my own garden." He took her hand and put the rose in it. "When I picked it, it occurred to me how much the two of you are alike."

"Oh?" The note of teasing in his voice raised Jenny's guard. "And how's that?"

"Two long-stemmed beauties... with thorns."

"Oh." Jenny supposed she could handle that. She ran a finger over the stem. "No thorns here."

"That's because I removed them."

Jenny found the look that accompanied that statement too smug to ignore. "If you think you can remove *my* thorns next, bud, you're in the wrong garden."

"Think so?" Eyes gleaming, David chucked her under the chin.

The patronizing gesture set Jenny's teeth on edge. "I *know* so." Arrogant...*male!* And why suddenly couldn't she think of a fittingly scathing epithet?

At odds with herself and David, not sure why and not really caring, she pushed past him. Leaving him to find his own way into the kitchen, she ran upstairs.

The door of her room clicked shut behind her, and she leaned back against it. Her heart was racing all out of proportion to the minimal effort it had taken to run up the short flight of stairs. It was him, of course, David Waterman—as able to upset and unsettle her as ever.

Jenny looked moodily down at the rose in her hand, then lifted it to her nose while her gaze idly surveyed the room. She saw ruffled curtains and a matching bedspread, a dainty dresser and vanity, some stuffed toys, a shelf of books. And everywhere photos of herself and Russell.

Russ. Lowering the flower, she pushed away from the door with a sigh. It occurred to her that Russ had never given her flowers. He'd never given her anything, really. Of course, she hadn't expected him to, she hastened to assure herself. She'd known he loved her even without fancy gifts. Or fancy words, a small voice reminded her.

Impatient with her thoughts, she dropped the rose onto the bed and went to shower.

She deliberately took her time. In order to keep her thoughts in line, she sang at the top of her lungs, concentrating on getting the lyrics just right.

"'On top of old Smoooo-keeee,'" she sang, in turn lathering and rinsing, and shaving her legs for good measure. "All covered in snoooow." Lifting first one foot, then the other, she scrubbed at her toenails. "I met my true loverr..."

Leaning back from the hips, she let the water cascade down her hair and face for a final rinse.

Russell hadn't been her lover very often. And on those few and awkward occasions when he had been, the act had never met with Jenny's expectations. This, she had thought, this groping and fumbling on the back seat of his car, was *it*? The ecstasy she'd read about, dreamed about, saw hinted at in the movies?

She'd look at David Waterman, note the adoring glances he collected like other guys collected stamps, and she'd wonder...

Oh, hell. Her movements jerky, Jenny turned off the water and stepped out of the shower. These days she wondered no more. She *knew*. She knew that David Waterman would not be a disappointment when it came to doing... *it*. Heck, he'd had enough practice, hadn't he?

Grimly she toweled herself dry. Furiously she told herself she was crazy. After all the emotional wounds she and David had inflicted on each other in the course of their reluctant association, and with all the dichotomous feelings he stirred in her now, how could she even remotely imagine they could ever be friends?

Or... more?

When Jenny came downstairs twenty minutes later, smells of roasting chicken from the kitchen and voices from the living room beckoned to her. With distinct reluctance, she veered off toward the latter.

"Hi, Pop."

Frank Dalton was on his knees next to David, in front of the TV. Bea was hovering over them.

"Hi, yourself." The smile Frank gave Jenny was pre-occupied. "Dave's explaining how to set my new VCR," he said, already turning back to the business at hand. "It's the very latest model, you know. So, Davey, you were say-ing...?"

Well familiar with Frank's ineptitude with things me-chanical, Jenny and Beatrice exchanged amused glances.

"Frank's one of those who'll only pick up a manual when all else fails," Bea teased.

"Manual, shmanual, who can read the things?"

"Lucky for you, then, that David's always been the mechanical type," Jenny said.

"You mean as opposed to the intellectual type?" David interjected.

"If the shoe fits." Jenny was itching for a fight with David. "Why is it you always put the worst interpretation on everything I say?" she demanded.

"With you, interpretation isn't needed, Stork," he shot back. "You always make damn sure your meaning's crys-tal clear."

"Are you saying I meant to insult you?"

"Don't you usually?"

"Only when provoked—"

"Look," Frank interrupted impatiently. "Could you kids continue this fight on your own time? My knees're aching...."

"And dinner'll be ready in fifteen minutes," Bea has-tened to add, ushering Jenny out of the room. "Come help me make the salad, hon."

Dinner was just like old times. Beatrice was doing all the talking, Jenny and David exchanged fulminating glances across the table, and Frank placidly ate. Preoccupied as she was with showing David that she really didn't care *how* he chose to interpret her remarks, Jenny didn't immediately realize she had become the focus of Bea's monologue. It took David's expression of malicious glee to alert her.

Her gaze swiveled to Bea's stern one. "What?"

"I said, I found it most upsetting to hear you declare on national television that you're glad to be single. How could you say a thing like that?"

"Because it's true?" Jenny hazarded with a feeble attempt at humor. The last thing she wanted was to get embroiled in a discussion of her marital preferences with David Waterman in the room.

"It's not!" Distressed, Bea dropped her fork. "You're not glad. You're not content." The flat of her hand slapping the table punctuated each pronouncement. "I say, you're afraid!"

Cheeks flushed, her fierce expression dared Jenny to deny it.

About to do just that, Jenny inhaled, but Bea wasn't through yet.

"What is wrong with today's young people that they can't make a commitment," she demanded of the table at large. "They date, they dally, they *cohabit*. You!" Her gaze swung to the other side and nailed David. "Why, pray tell, are you still single at thirty-two years of age?"

Jenny was delighted to find someone other than herself fidgeting beneath Beatrice's accusing glare for a change. She was especially glad to have it be David Waterman and eagerly seized the chance to score another point off him.

"Yes, David," she needled sweetly. "With the myriad of women who've no doubt paraded through your be—"

She broke off, sent him an innocent smile and corrected, "Through your *life*—why *is* that?"

David wasn't too proud of the way he'd been acting toward Jenny but seemed unable to stop himself. When she'd walked into that living room—squeaky-clean and more fragrant than the most precious rose in his garden—he'd been swamped by a deluge of such powerful feelings they'd scared him to death. And he'd reacted the way he always reacted to fear: with aggression.

The tactic had worked, too, because it had brought out Storky Jones's true nature and poison tongue, both of which he'd forgotten about for a couple of days.

Trading gibes with her, watching her squirm beneath Bea's first degree, he'd been caught off guard by Bea's abrupt change of focus. He'd been too busy looking forward to watching Jenny try to wiggle out of Bea's clutches to immediately realize that he had, in fact, become the victim.

A quick glance at Jenny, as well as the things she'd said, left no doubt but that she relished the opportunity to now see *him* squirm. Fat chance, Stork!

Leaning back in his chair, he gave Bea his best smile. "Why is that, you ask? Well, I'll tell you. It's because most of today's women are either too beautiful or too smart. They intimidate a man." He leaned forward to warmly cover her hand with his. "Guess they don't make 'em like you anymore, sweetheart."

Bea flushed and said, "Posh," but she was clearly gratified.

Frank said, beaming, "I think he's right, Mother."

And Jenny? Driving home, David relived the moment with great relish.

Derision had been clearly readable in Storky Jones's delft blue eyes before she'd lowered her lashes and refused to look his way again for the rest of the meal. Derision, and something else, too. Disappointment? Accusation?

Hell.

Grimly David negotiated the narrow turn into his gravel driveway with practiced ease. He'd known this friendship thing wasn't going to work between them. She was too damn touchy, and too many other things, too. Things he didn't want to deal with, complicated things that would only mess up his life. Who needed it?

Getting out of his prized Corvette, David took time to cover it with a tarpaulin, all the while cursing himself for having brought Jenny that rose. He'd bought a bouquet of flowers for Bea, and he'd told himself it would be rude not to have something for Jenny, too.

Bull!

The fact of the matter was, he'd brought the thing because he'd let that damn auction, one champagne-and-rumba-induced lip-lock, and a niggling sense of guilt about Russell blind him to the fact that he and she could never mesh.

Become friends with Storky Jones? Or more?

David stormed into the house and slammed the door. He'd as soon cuddle up with a *real* shrew—the furry kind.

Chapter Five

Jenny always had lunch with Georgette on Wednesdays. She usually looked forward to it, because it was invariably a lively couple of hours. No one would ever accuse Georgette Myerson of being dull.

Dull, no, Jenny reflected, dourly contemplating the yellow rose in the bud vase on her office desk. Nosy, yes. She just knew that during today's lunch she'd be in for a quizzing about her date with David Waterman, and, worse, if she gave even the tiniest hint of having warmed toward the man, she'd be subjected to yet another attempt at matchmaking.

Well, she darn well had *not* warmed toward him, so the latter would hardly become a problem.

Jenny glared at the flower and reiterated that not only hadn't she warmed toward him, she wouldn't let one lousy dethorned rosebud make her lose sight of the fact that, left in each other's company for more than minutes at a time, behaviors and attitudes from the past most unpleasantly reared their ugly heads.

He was obviously under the impression that she still thought of him as a dim-witted jock, which, of course, wasn't the case at all. On the other hand, she *knew* — hadn't he made it clear right there at the Dalton dinner table? — that he still considered *her* an unattractive egghead, a woman too smart for a man to love.

Jenny picked up the vase, moodily eyeing its lone occupant. Long-stemmed beauties, David had said she and this rose were. It hadn't sounded as if he thought her so all-fired ugly....

Impatient with what she considered a pathetic need on her part to read more into David's remark than he'd intended, Jenny cut herself short. They'd been pretty words, a practiced line meant to charm, nothing more. Wasn't he a Don Juan of long standing? And hadn't she witnessed him in action countless times years ago?

She got up and carried the vase out to the front office.

"It's giving me a headache," she said in response to Ruth's questioning look.

"That's funny." Ruth sniffed. "There isn't any scent that I can smell. Your nose must be better than mine."

"Must be." Jenny shrugged into her raincoat. "I'm out of here."

"Lunch?"

"Yep."

"Have fun."

"Right." Wiggling her fingers in a breezy farewell, Jenny left the office.

Any fun she might have hoped to have was reduced to wishful thinking the minute she spotted David in the restaurant. Every inch the businessman in a charcoal-gray suit, light blue shirt and muted tie, he was seated with three similarly attired men a couple of tables down from the booth in which Georgette sat. To make matters worse, there was no chair that would have allowed Jenny to keep her back to David, only a curved, upholstered bench seat facing the room.

Good manners—and the watchful Georgette—required that she acknowledge him, and she did so with a nod and the ghost of a restrained smile.

"Hi, Georgette." Though David's silent response to Jenny's greeting had been as full of reserve as hers, Jenny felt his eyes on her as she shrugged out of her coat and hung it on the provided peg before sliding into the booth. "Been waiting long?"

"A couple of minutes. I ordered us white wine."

"Thanks." With an air of busyness, Jenny fumbled for reading glasses in her purse, plunked them onto her nose and picked up the menu. In the act of opening it, her gaze flew to David of its own accord. He was still looking at her but with a frown now.

Oh, Lord.

Flushing crimson, she yanked off the glasses. She'd needed them to read since grade school, and he'd always said they made her look like an owl. Quickly she turned her face aside, only to find herself looking straight at Georgette.

Her friend had obviously been watching her ridiculous behavior, for she sat chin in palm, one long and flawlessly manicured fingernail thoughtfully tapping a snowy white tooth.

"What's going on?" she asked.

"How do you mean?"

Georgette gave that the reply it deserved. None.

"Oh, you mean David?" Jenny busied herself with the menu again, giving a breezy little laugh. "Why, nothing."

she made a mistake, she always did her best to
hen she did someone wrong, she always apol-

, she now owed David Waterman an apology
course, knowing what had to be done and ac-
the thing were two entirely different animals.
y the more distasteful a task, the more quickly
to get it out of the way, experience having
hat dreading the deed was usually tougher on
than the deed itself. In other words, the best
in this case would be to go over to David's ta-
en and there, ask to speak with him in private
nt and then say what had to be said.

thing in her rebelled against the idea. A. She
a chance to give any thought to what she might
him. B. There was Georgette to contend with.
hat if he said no, he didn't want to speak with
she'd be with egg on her face.

t'd be much better to do the thing in private so
d rebuff her, she could at least lick her wounds
audience.

ded to speak with him the next morning at his
siness.

unicipal airport, Waterman Aviation was hard
what appeared to be the office building, as well
ront of the hangar next to it, oversize letters
the name.

rked her compact car and walked over to the
f small airplanes tied up in front of the han-
uld see David in the middle of them with an-
an employee, she assumed, since both he and
dressed alike in light blue oxford shirts, navy
slacks. Both men were wearing aviator sun-

To her relief Georgette let that pass. "Did you two do
the auction date?"

"Yep," Jenny said into the menu.

Georgette reached over and pulled it down. "Am I to
assume by your—and David's—peculiar attitude that all
did not go well?"

Deprived of her hiding place, Jenny laid the menu aside
and sat up straight. "Everything went very well, actually.
We had declared a truce, you see."

"Ah." Georgette's brows rose as if in understanding.
"And now the truce is over, is that it?"

"Something like that."

The waiter brought their glasses of wine. They sipped,
but Georgette's gaze remained fixed on Jenny. "Want to
tell me about it?"

"Not especially." For as long as she could, Jenny kept
her own eyes on the glass she was carefully setting down.
Finally, with a sigh, she met her friend's patient gaze.
"Maybe. I don't know."

Shifting in the seat, she turned more fully toward Georgette. "The thing is, it's all tied up with the past, it's..."
She shrugged, frowning. "It's complicated."

"I'll try and keep up."

Jenny's quick smile was sheepish. "And probably asinine."

"Quit stalling."

"Well, all right. Remember I mentioned the night of the
auction that David and I go way back?"

Georgette nodded.

"Well, he was Russell's—my own lifelong friend and
later fiancé's—best friend."

"Uh-huh...?" Georgette prompted encouragingly when
Jenny paused.

"The trouble was, David and I were like cat and dog, always at each other, scratching and growling, going for blood...."

Jenny went on to describe their rocky relationship, as well as Russell's constant distress over it.

"The one thing he wanted more than anything," she said, winding down, "was for David and me to like each other. Well—"

Pausing, she remembered the Latin Club and their scorching kiss on the dance floor. A flame kindled in her midsection, and she had to clear her throat before she could speak again.

"The, uh, *date* ended so well," she continued haltingly, only too aware of the whopping understatement, "that, uh, David and I—well, we sort of agreed to try to be friends."

She fell silent, struck by something she'd just said. They had agreed to *try*.

Disconcerted, she bit her lip and looked blindly down at the napkin she'd twisted into a pretzel as she talked. *Had* she tried, honestly tried, yesterday evening at the Daltons'? Or wasn't it true that, at the first opportunity, she'd grabbed the chance to revert to form? Fighting with David was what she knew how to do; being friends with him, and coping with the manifold feelings he aroused, was a whole new—and pretty darn scary—ball game.

"So what happened?"

At Georgette's dry question, Jenny looked up. Her lip curled. "I forgot."

"You forgot what happened?"

"I forgot to try."

"I see."

Trouble was, Jenny did, too. She saw that it would probably be up to her to make the first move toward try-

---

ing again. After all, David
she probably owed it to Russ

She risked a sideways glan
wasn't looking at her. His fa
accustomed to seeing it, he w
thing one of his companions
nodded, or made some point
turn, intently listened to. It
considered noteworthy anythi
his opinions were respected.

With a jolt Jenny realized t
she had never respected either

That fact hit her in the head
it was as if, suddenly, some so
had been knocked away from
now she was able to see David
man, self-assured but not cock
sive; a man who was smart, bu
remotely the wise guy of her yo
demeanor.

Phew! Shaken, Jenny blew o
caught Georgette's interested
watch with a quick, sickly smile
late and I'm finding all this so
hungry work. Could we order?"

What she really wanted was
ments of peace during which she
her newfound insights. So, with
to say yea or nay, she picked up
appeared behind it. Everything
blur without her glasses on, but
thing on her mind just then, it di

Jenny was thinking, considerir
she had her share of faults, but ex

glasses on this warm and sunny late spring day and seemed deeply involved in their discussion.

Not wishing to interrupt, Jenny strolled along the periphery of the parked planes while she waited for David to be free. She'd never been comfortable around the small flying machines, had always avoided them as much as possible, in fact. But she could recognize a Cessna 152 when she saw one, mostly because it was the model in which Russell had learned to fly, and because pictures of it had been all over his room.

Even inside his wallet, she'd always somewhat resentfully suspected, right in the place where other guys carried photos of their sweethearts.

She approached the two-seater with a mixture of curiosity and trepidation. Gingerly, as if it might scorch her hand, she touched the shiny enamel of its white-and-orange paintwork. Cool, smooth. Harmless.

Thinking the word made her smile at her foolishness in expecting it to be otherwise, and, having come this far, she ducked beneath the wing to peer inside the cockpit.

Leather seats, a bunch of knobs and dials, two steering wheels. Except that each seemed to be only the bottom half of a wheel.

"Buy a plane, ma'am?"

Jenny started as if caught doing something illicit and, quickly stepping away from the window, bumped her head on the strut supporting the wing. Rubbing the sore spot, she turned to send a look of mild chagrin toward David, who had come to stand at the nose of the plane. He was watching her, his mouth unsmiling, the expression in his eyes hidden behind the mirrored glasses.

"Buying, selling, leasing, too—Waterman is the place for you," he recited, still deadpan, when she didn't reply to his question. "Catchy, don't you think?"

"Practically inspired." Relieved because the mature David obviously didn't believe in holding grudges any more than the youthful David had, Jenny ventured a tentative smile. "Who writes your advertising copy?"

"I do."

"Ah." Keeping her head and shoulders bent, she moved toward him, straightening once she was clear of the wing. "It shows."

David closed the gap between them further. His brows arched above the wire rims of his shades. "I think I'm insulted."

"Oh, no!" Jenny's expression of horror was only partially feigned. That's all she needed, she thought, to put her foot in it all over again. "I came to make peace, not start another skirmish."

"I see."

Jenny wished she could, too, but his lips remained uncurved and his shaded eyes reflected only herself, looking nervous. She waited, hoping he'd say something else, but all he did was continue to stand there. It seemed, as far as he was concerned, the ball was back in her court.

"I wondered if maybe we could give this friendship thing another try," she finally said.

At that his lips first compressed, then pursed, as if he were weighing her words and their possible consequences before answering. Turning his head, he idly ran a hand along the plane's nose the way an equestrian might stroke the muzzle of his horse.

"Russ ever take you up in one of these?" he asked.

Disconcerted, because she'd expected an acknowledgment of her olive branch instead of this seemingly idle question, Jenny only mutely shook her head. Then, realizing that he wasn't looking at her, she cleared her throat and said, "No," and, after a moment, added, "but then I never wanted him to."

"Would you go up with me?"

As he asked, he took off his sunglasses and looked at her, though he might as well have kept them on because she still couldn't tell what he was thinking.

Panic-stricken, she was thinking, *Oh, no! Help!*

But there was something in the way he stood, in the slight tilt of his head and carefully neutral expression, that left her with the sense that the possibility of friendship between them might well hinge on the kind of reply she made.

In an agony of indecision about how best to handle this, momentarily struck dumb by unreasoning panic and wishing he'd ask anything of her but that, Jenny mutely stared at him for several charged seconds.

She realized she'd waited too long when she saw a flash of pain briefly darken his eyes before he slipped the shades back in front of them and hid them. One corner of his mouth quirked in a crooked smile.

"The FAA wouldn't be letting me operate this business and fly charters, Jen," he said quietly, his voice roughened by emotion, "if they thought I'd caused a fatal accident."

It took a moment for the words to get past the inner war she'd been waging against her cowardice, but when they did, and their meaning sank in, she was horrified.

And she found her voice. "David," she implored, reaching out to touch him. "I told you I don't think that accident was your fault. I don't," she repeated, feeling the tension in the muscled arm beneath her hand. "The only reason I hesitated just now was that I—"

She broke off with a shake of the head and a rueful smile. "I was hoping you'd ask me," she fibbed. Anything to make him feel better! "And when you did I . . . I wondered if I'd been too obvious about it, that's all."

The way one of his brows arched above the sunglasses and the way his lips pursed again made clear to Jenny that he wasn't altogether convinced by her breathless declaration.

So she stuck a bright smile on her face, unobtrusively crossed her fingers and said, "Really. I'd love to go up. Some other time."

His other brow rose. "What's wrong with right now? I need to test this baby here anyway."

"Gosh." Appalled, Jenny backed up a step. "Gee, I don't know, David . . ." She glanced at her watch, then worriedly back up at him. "It's getting awfully late, you know. I only came to—"

"Aw, come on, Jen." David gripped her around the shoulders and gave her an encouraging squeeze. On a logical level he knew he shouldn't be trying to talk Jenny into going up with him, but then logic didn't have anything to do with whatever he did around Storky Jones.

Her protestations notwithstanding, in his heart of hearts he'd always been sure she blamed him for Russell's death. More, he was convinced that, in *her* heart of hearts, Jenny wished he'd been the one who'd died instead of Russ. And he guessed the reason he wanted so badly to have her fly with him today was maybe to show her what a responsible and capable pilot he really was. Too responsible and capable to have crashed a plane through negligence of some sort, even then.

He might have been a wild kind of kid, full of the devil and not above taking chances, but never while flying. Never. If she went up with him today, it'd be an act of faith on her part and, after all the bickering and the hurt and the insults they'd exchanged, he found he needed that from her if they were ever to be the kind of . . . *friends* he suddenly knew he wanted them to be.

"Come on," he urged again. "I'm just going to fly the pattern a couple of times to make sure this little crate is doing what it's supposed to. There's no wind, no turbulence." Taking off his glasses, he squinted at her. "You scared?"

Jenny pulled a face. "As a matter of fact, yes."

David cupped her cheek and gently forced her to look into his eyes. "Trust me, Jen," he said, his voice a husky rasp because the apprehension he read in her eyes caused a surge of tenderness to tighten his throat. "Trust me."

Unable to think of a single reason not to, barely able to think at all beneath David's warm scrutiny, Jenny dragged a shaky breath past the wobble of her tentative smile.

"I do," she said, and found she really meant it.

The half circle of David's arm around her shoulder tightened, drawing her closer still against his side. "Then you'll come?"

Jenny's nod was almost imperceptible, but her voice, though as soft and low as his, was firm. "Yes."

And as their gazes continued to hold, they both knew that some indefinable but vitally important barrier between them had been breached.

"Hey, boss!"

David was visibly, and, to Jenny, gratifyingly, reluctant to acknowledge and respond to the voice that was hailing him. Very slowly, keeping his eyes linked with Jenny's for as long as possible and her body aligned with his, he turned his head toward the caller. Quite automatically, Jenny followed suit.

"What is it?" David barked.

"Phone call."

"Have Martha take a message."

"She did, and it's urgent."

The man Jenny'd seen talking with David when she first got to Waterman Aviation was offering an apologetic smile. Gingerly he stepped up to them. He was middle-aged and balding, with a likable face and a burgeoning potbelly.

"Excuse me, ma'am. Dave."

"Jenny," David said resignedly, "meet Bert Kastell, my senior pilot. Bert, Eugenie Jones, a very dear friend of mine."

Warmed to the core by that appellation, Jenny accepted the older man's outstretched hand and shook it. "Mr. Kastell."

"Bert'll do just fine, ma'am."

"Bert, then. And I'm Jenny."

Bert's smile grew. "Pleasure to meet you, Jenny."

Watching Jenny and his senior pilot beam at each other made David feel strangely left out. Darn it, he groused, frowning, what with their newfound...*whatever*, he wanted Jenny to himself for a while.

"Bert," he prompted none too gently. "The message?"

"Oh."

David's obvious impatience with the interruption and Bert's chagrined flush at having been caught making cow eyes at her made Jenny feel more feminine and desirable than she ever remembered feeling. Heady with it, she gently ducked out of David's now relaxed hold.

"Excuse me," she said, grinning up at him, "but is there a rest room in one of these?" She touched the 152.

Bert guffawed while David only narrowed his eyes at her.

"Right." Including Bert in her grin, she backed away. "In that case I'd better go find one on the ground before I go flying, hadn't I?"

"In the office," David called after her.

Jenny waved acknowledgment without turning.

"This better be good," David said to Bert.

Bert shrugged. "I don't know about good or bad, I only know what Martha said to tell you."

"Which is?"

"If you want that loan, the bankers need to see you pronto."

So much for taking Jenny up for a spin, David thought on a quick sigh. So much for testing her faith, her trust....

"I was going to take 4398 Kilo here—" he once more patted the nose of the little Cessna next to which they were standing "—and my friend Jenny up for a spin," he told Bert, his tone not nearly as regretful as he was feeling, "but I guess we'd better put that off for another day."

Bert nodded. "Yeah, if we want that loan..."

"And we do, so get one of the instructors to take the Cessna through its paces, would you?"

"Right."

"Okay." Firmly shoving aside his momentary reluctance to assume his responsibilities as a businessman and employer, David briskly set out toward the office with Bert falling into step beside him. His mind already weighing means and alternatives, he said, "Did Martha say if they sounded positive?"

"Nope."

"Negative?"

"Nope." Bert, panting from the exertion of trying to keep up with David's longer stride, shot him a sideways glance. "But you know how bankers are, Dave. They give nothing away. We're sound, though, aren't we?"

Grimly David shrugged. "As sound as any of us are in today's economy." He glanced at Bert and caught a worried frown. "Of course, we're sound," he assured the older man. "And at lunch yesterday, they seemed very willing." Stepping up to the front door of his office building and holding the door for Bert, he added, "They'll help us get that dealership, so you just fly while I do the worrying."

Inside the reception area they encountered Jenny, coming out of the rest room. Bert discreetly kept going when David stopped in front of her, gripped both of her shoulders and brought his face close to hers. "Can you stand it?" he quipped, well aware of what her decision to go fly with him had cost her, and of the relief she'd no doubt feel at being handed a reprieve. "I'm going to have to give you a rain check on the flight around the pattern. Unless you want to go up with whoever does that test flight for me?"

"No, no..."

At her too-quick protestation, he grinned and gave in to an urge that had grown steadily throughout their encounter. He kissed her. Full on the lips, quickly, with fondness. But only because he knew it was too soon for passion—there were too many unknowns still to be explored between them and this time he was determined not to rush.

And the bankers were waiting. "Can I call you?"

Jenny smiled, trying to keep her accelerated heartbeat and her patent relief at not having to fly, in check. "Of course."

"Tonight?"

"Tomorrow would be better."

"Morning?"

"Sounds good."

It took a conscious act of will on David's part to let go of her shoulders. "Talk to you then." He backed away.

Her gaze still connected to his, Jenny nodded. "All right."

David watched her walk away, then strode toward his office.

Chapter Six

"Yes, Mother. Of course, I'd be delighted if you came for a visit. Next month? No? August. All right, let me see..."

With her one free hand Jenny sifted through the clutter of books and papers on her desk, trying to find a calendar.

"Here we are." She wedged the phone between ear and hunched shoulder—how was it that other people, like Ruth out front, for instance, were able to make that look so easy?—and flipped some pages. "About when in August were you thinking, Mother? Middle-ish. Uh-huh...yes. I see. No, I don't see a problem with that."

The door opened right on the heels of the knock Jenny heard. Georgette's head appeared. Her eyes questioned, Is it okay to come in?

The nod with which Jenny accompanied her quick wave of invitation dislodged the phone. Noisily it clattered to the desk.

Meeting Georgette's amused gaze with a sigh of vexation about her clumsiness, Jenny picked the thing up but held it in hand. "Sorry. I dropped it, yes. Someone came in. A friend." She rolled her eyes at Georgette. "No, Mother, not a man."

Albeit blessedly long-distance, Rosalie Jones was every bit as dedicated to fixing Jenny up with a mate as was Beatrice Dalton. Rosalie's position was that no woman over thirty—no matter what her job or career or personal philosophy—had any business living alone. She and Jenny had never been close, Rosalie had always been too stern a taskmaster to allow something like friendship to flourish between them, the way it had between Jenny and her father.

"So, we're saying the sixteenth?" Jenny now prompted, not only to steer the conversation away from potentially choppy waters, but also to wind it down. "A Wednesday. Got it. Right. Good. Gotta go, Mother. Kiss for Dad. Bye."

Clicking the Reset with her thumb, she broke the connection and laid the portable down. *"Phew!"*

She sagged, sending Georgette a comically helpless look. "Is your mother as relentless as mine?"

"About mating, no." Georgette was idly wandering around Jenny's spacious office, touching here, looking there. She was her usual stunning self in a pale peach linen suit, her auburn mane artfully scrunched and tousled, her delicate facial features highlighted to perfection.

If I were a jealous, competitive sort of female, Jenny thought, fondly eyeing her glamorous friend, I'd hate her!

"My career, however, is another matter. Mother is into success. Never having had any of her own—all of her four marriages failed and work is a naughty four-letter word—

she vicariously basks in mine. And so it's, push, push, push ... the consummate stage mother!''

Georgette had come to a halt near the conversational corner—a couch and two chairs grouped around a low coffee table—where Jenny sat with clients who needed to discuss lengthy or complicated translating projects. At each end of the sofa a small table supported a lamp, as well as assorted framed photographs.

Bending, Georgette peered at several, then picked one up and, straightening, studied it more closely.

Jenny could tell by the frame that it was the one of Russell, David and herself. Her father had snapped it in front of their house. They were eighteen, and all three of them jean-clad and scruffy after the rough-and-tumble game of touch football on their lawn the guys had talked her into. Each of them had an arm draped across her shoulders, sandwiching her between their bodies.

"You don't look here as if you hated the guy," Georgette said, lowering the picture. *"Au contraire!"*

In spite of herself, Jenny flushed in response to the arch look her friend tossed her. She recalled how acutely aware of David's tough, athletic physique she'd been, and how she'd been comparing the feel of it to the feel of Russell's lean frame....

"If Dad had shot the thing five minutes later, you wouldn't be saying that."

Which was true, because David had felt called upon to throw one of his usual taunts her way. Something about feeling punctured like a pincushion from all the times Jenny had stabbed her sharp elbows and skinny body into him during the game. Jenny had been livid and mortified, all the more so because of her own distressingly breathless reaction to body contact with him.

Drawing herself up in her chair, she gave a ruefully reminiscent chuckle. "I'm afraid that's how it always was with us. Tiny lulls, followed by gigantic squalls." She shook her head, frowning. "Who can figure it?"

"I can." Georgette set the photo down and, sauntering over to the desk, gave Jenny a bright smile. "Chemistry 101."

"I see," Jenny said dryly, and, tapping a finger against her teeth Georgette-style, pretended to think. "Now what do I remember from that course? I've got it," she exclaimed, slapping her palm onto her desk. "Ammonia and chlorine. You mix those suckers and it's hold your nose and look out, Charlie!" She laughed. "You're a genius, Georgette."

"All right," Georgette conceded blithely, "so maybe it's not chemistry. What's his sign?"

"Sign?" Oh, brother, Jenny thought. "The only sign of his I've seen says Waterman Aviation."

"Cute." Georgette's narrowed glare conveyed displeasure at Jenny's levity. "His *birth* sign, if you please."

"Oh, that." Jenny couldn't hide a grin. Did people really still ask that these days? she wondered with considerable amusement. "I don't know."

"You don't know!" Georgette repeated, clearly appalled. "You've known this man forever and you don't know his birthday? That's terrible!"

It was terrible, wasn't it? Jenny conceded. "The subject never came up," she said, wondering how it was that it hadn't.

"So what are you?" asked Georgette.

"Me. March tenth, Pisces. Why?"

"Hmm." Georgette looked thoughtful. "In that case, a Cancer male would be your best bet, mate-wise," she said after a while.

Jenny silently rolled her eyes.

"But the way you two act around each other," Georgette went on, undeterred, "I'm positive that's not David's sign." Highly entertained, Jenny watched her friend pace a few steps while she deliberated, then stop and declare, "I've got it!"

"Let's pray it's not catching," Jenny murmured, earning herself another reproachful glance.

"David Waterman is a Pisces, too," Georgette stated firmly. "Has to be."

"Oh?"

"Of course. Which is exactly why you're at each other all the time. You're too much alike."

Oh, brother! For an instant Jenny could only stare at Georgette, dumbfounded. She and David Waterman, *alike?* She broke into peals of laughter. "Now I've heard everything."

"Go ahead, laugh." Georgette blithely studied her impeccably manicured nails. "I know what I know."

"And I'd like to know what brought you here this morning," Jenny countered, still shaking her head and chuckling. "Unlike you I'm not a famous *personality*. I've got to work for a living."

"Well." Clearly miffed by Jenny's blatant skepticism of her theories, Georgette pulled a book out of her purse and dropped it onto the desk. "Your work is precisely why I came. I promised Billy I'd see you got this back."

"Really?" A quick glance at the book identified it as an old dictionary she had lent Bill Shafer to help him with the reading of an antique German work. Its outdated phrasing had given him trouble. "That was nice of you, but hardly necessary, considering I only gave it to him three days ago and told him I was in no hurry to get it back."

She regarded Georgette with a mixture of skepticism and expectation. "So what really brought you?"

"All right." Georgette shrugged, unrepentant. "After yesterday's lunch I was—understandably, you'll admit—curious."

The phone rang.

"Excuse me." Jenny picked it up. "Ruth, can you hold my calls. I— Oh."

David Waterman.

Jenny flushed as her heart did an unexpected flip-flop before settling into an erratic beat. "All right, put him on."

Acutely conscious of being the subject of Georgette's very interested study, she swiveled the chair so that it faced the other way, and lowered her voice. "Hi! No, I'm fine, it's just that—"

Georgette rounded the desk and, gleefully ogling and blatantly eavesdropping, planted herself in front of Jenny, who promptly spun the chair back the other way.

"I'm kind of tied up right at the moment. Sunday?"

She glared at Georgette, who'd hastened to resume her position in front of the desk.

"Sure, sounds like fun. I'd love to. All right, then. So am I. Bye." She clicked off the phone. "Georgette Myerson, you are the most—"

"Ciao, darling, gotta run." Laughing, Georgette wiggled her fingers and hurried out the door, only to instantly stick her head back in. "I got what I came for, thanks."

Grinning, she crooned a terrible imitation of Bing Crosby singing to Grace Kelly in *High Society*, "...true love, true lo-o-ve..."

Jenny leaped to her feet, bent on retribution. The door fell shut, muffling but not quite shutting out the receding

strains of Georgette's off-key singing and Ruth's delighted laughter.

David had initially said he'd come by for her around ten-
thirty in the morning, but then, yesterday, Jenny had suf-
fered an attack of anxiety and second thoughts. She had
reasoned that it would be unsettling enough to just *be* in
David's house, on his turf, so to speak, for the entire day
without having to be at his mercy with regard to transpor-
tation, too. After all, their cease-fire record could not be
called the best in anybody's book, so who was she to say
they wouldn't be ending this day with another skirmish?
At least, if she had her own wheels, she could just up and
leave.

And so Jenny had called him yesterday, having in-
vented an errand she'd have to run prior to their ap-
pointed time. Since it would bring her near his
neighborhood anyway, et cetera, had been her line.

An excuse, pure and simple.

David had been tactful enough not to ask what kind of
an errand, for which she was grateful because, even though
she'd had an answer ready, she hated to lie any more than
necessary. Besides which, by the time she'd called him
she'd begun to feel a little foolish about her apprehen-
sions, but by then she'd been committed to her story, and
so she'd merely written down his address and directions
and let it go at that.

Games, Jenny thought. And here she'd prided herself on
having grown beyond the need for them.

Creeping along Lake Washington Boulevard, the slip of
paper with David's address and directions in hand, she
figured his house had to be that little one, up the road there
three houses. The others, like most of the homes with

properties right on Lake Washington, were somehow grander and showier than she'd expected David's to be.

It wasn't that she thought he couldn't afford one of those—for all she knew his business might have made him millions, and even a modest house on the lake didn't come cheap, after all. No, it had to do with her newfound perception of him. Call it feminine intuition, whatever, she just somehow knew now that for all the flashy brashness of his yesteryears, and in spite of his current demeanor of self-assured masculinity, inside David Waterman was a basically unassuming sort of guy. And his house would reflect that.

Number 3521. Pulling the steering wheel in a hard left in order to negotiate the sharp turn into the gravel driveway, Jenny permitted herself a small, self-satisfied smile. She'd been right. This tiny clapboard house, little more than a cottage, was David's. And, with its patches of peeling paint and bleached-out woodwork, it was definitely unassuming.

But the potential!

Setting the hand brake and killing the engine, Jenny took in the dilapidated structure, the weed-infested lawn and scraggly rosebushes, the tarpaulin covering a car that was probably a junker. There'd always been at least one of those littering the yard of the Watermans home two doors down from hers. Not for young David a modest secondhand sedan like the one that had been Russell's first car. Oh, no. David had always had some exotic wreck or other in the works, with several more around just for parts.

Well, Jenny noted, that wasn't the case here, at least. Things were shabby, yes, but also decidedly neat. The windows of the house sparkled, the sorry lawn was precisely edged. And next to the decently covered supposed junker, a freshly washed, late-model minivan was parked

on the gravel. Waterman Aviation was emblazoned along
its sides.

Ah, yes, Jenny thought, the tax-deductible company
wheels! Her smirk was short-lived, however—only long
enough for her to remind herself that she, too, was not
above deducting mileage on her car when she used it for
business, and that there was nothing wrong with that.

Why was it so consistently difficult for her to discard her
outdated stereotype of David Waterman as the bad guy?

Impatient with herself, Jenny got out of the car—just as
the scratched-up and faded front door swung wide. A
huge, tattered black cat shot out and around the corner of
the house. And then there was David, breathtaking in
frayed cutoffs and on old football jersey, his feet, inside
scuffed docksiders, bare. His hair looked as if it had only
been finger-combed, and his facial expression was homi-
cidal.

"And stay out," he hollered after the fleeing feline, apparently unaware that Jenny had arrived.

Which was no wonder, Jenny thought wryly, considering the decibel level of the music blasting from his house.

He was muttering to himself, his expression black, and
about to close the door again when he caught sight of her
standing next to her car in his driveway.

Like sun emerging from behind a thunderhead, his slow
smile crept out to erase the frown and brighten his eyes.

"Hi!" He let go of the door and walked toward her.

Jenny saw that he had a kitchen towel draped over one
shoulder and a long chef's knife in one hand. Pointing to
it, glad to have chanced upon a subject she could be airy
about in spite of her rattled nerves, she said, "No wonder
that cat ran for its life."

His eyes followed the direction of hers. He chuckled. "Tempting thought, now that you mention it."

Jenny laughed, too. "What'd she do?"

"He." David was now standing right in front of her, so close the tantalizing fragrance of fried bacon that clung to him made Jenny salivate.

At least she told herself it was the bacon.

"Damned fleabag gobbled up the chicken livers I'd just cooked and chopped for our omelet."

Bless you, cat.

David must have read the thought in her eyes. "You don't like chicken livers?"

"Well..." Jenny inwardly squirmed. Here he was nice enough to have her over and cook brunch.... "As a matter of fact—" How to put it politely? She caught the amused glint in his eye and opted for the unadulterated truth. *"Yuck!"*

"And here you always claimed we had nothing in common!" David laughed, clasping her shoulders while he steered her toward the house. "Never could stand the slimy things myself."

"Then why on earth were you cooking them?" Jenny exclaimed, trying not to be unnerved by his casual touch and the feel of his hips bumping against hers as they walked.

"Well now, there's a question." David grinned down at her. "And the answer has to do with preconditioning. Or preconceptions. Whatever. You're a classy woman, you've lived abroad...." He shrugged. "I figured chicken livers, beluga caviar, all that stuff'd probably be staples in your diet."

Jenny stopped walking. "Please tell me you didn't get caviar."

"I didn't." Close as they were, their bodies absorbed each other's heartbeats. Their gazes roamed across each other's face with all the fresh curiosity of explorers tracing new territories. Their breaths mingled as they smiled at each other. "But only because the corner grocery store didn't carry it."

"Oh, David..."

What Jenny had intended as a lighthearted dismissal of his foolish misconceptions about her tastes instead came out as a breathless whisper.

And as her eyes roamed to his lips, David echoed an equally ragged, "Oh, Jen..."

A bloodcurdling yowl, followed by fierce barking, sundered, like a thunderclap, the charged air between them. As they jumped apart, a dark streak shot through the space between their feet with a frantically barking Saint Bernard lumbering after it in hot pursuit.

David began to laugh. "Way to go, Sly."

"Sly?" Jenny pressed a hand to her racing heart, thoroughly shaken, though more from the sighing exchange she'd had with David than from the cat-and-dog sideshow. "Which one is Sly?"

"My cat." Still chuckling, moving briskly now, David led the way into the house. "Must've gotten into poor old Bernie's chow again."

"Your Sly sounds like quite the opportunist to me."

They were in the house now, and Jenny had to practically shout that observation to be heard above the blaring music. She crashed into David as he suddenly stopped and turned. His hands clasped her upper arms.

"Well, you know what they say," he murmured, all the laughter gone from his face. "Like master, like cat."

He dropped a soft kiss onto her lips before Jenny could even think of avoiding it. "Welcome to my parlor, Storky."

Jenny was by no means the first woman David had ever entertained in his home, but she was, he admitted wryly to himself, the first one he'd ever been nervous about.

He wanted to impress her, was what it was, of course. He wanted her to look around, see his books, hear his music, and realize that there was more to him than the dumb jock facade she'd never taken the time to penetrate.

What he had not wanted—no, scratch that. What he had not *intended* to do this morning was to kiss her. But, of course, he'd done it anyway. Stupid, he told himself angrily as he watched her take a couple of aimless steps toward the living room in an obvious struggle to regain some emotional equilibrium.

He briefly considered apologizing but decided that would probably just make things worse.

"So..." Small talk to the rescue. "What do you think?" He made a sweeping gesture and tried to sound offhand.

"Very nice."

Following her gaze with his, seeing the room through her eyes, David wished he'd taken more care with decorating. His stuff was nice enough, as far as it went. Oak coffee and side tables, a tan leather couch and two chairs. Lamps and a few objets d'art from a trip he'd taken to Japan a few years ago.

Of course, the gunmetal gray file cabinet and paper-littered desk in the corner kind of jarred. And the smell of paint and varnish seemed stronger with her here, too, he thought critically. It had only been two weeks since he'd finished painting the walls and refinishing the hardwood floor.

"Not much, but it's home," he quipped, as always using glibness to hide his vulnerabilities. "I'm a bachelor, what can I say?"

"I like it," Jenny protested sincerely, then gestured with a look of apology toward the shelf arrangement along one wall, which housed his prized stereo components. "But could we turn that down, do you think?"

"That's jazz, you know," David said, a little defensively, and just in case Jenny hadn't realized his tastes had grown beyond the pounding acid rock with which he'd used to bombard his and every neighbor's eardrums in his younger days. He lowered the volume.

"Thanks." Jenny smiled at him. "It's great stuff, but a little hard for me to overshout."

She wandered over to the expanse of glass that made up the entire wall facing the lake. A deep, upholstered window seat was below the length of the window.

Propping herself on it on one knee, Jenny drank in the view for long, silent moments.

"You're so lucky to have this place," she exclaimed when she finally turned her shining eyes back toward David. "Do you know that?"

"Boy, do I."

Warmed by her enthusiasm, pleased out of all proportion by her approval of his view, David caught her hand in his free one and tugged her along behind him.

"You know, I used to drive by this place every day for almost a year, hoping and praying I'd get enough money together for a down payment before they leveled the thing.

"They did that to all the other old houses along here, you see," he elaborated, "in order to put up those man-sions out there. As I found out, the only reason this place stayed intact was that the lot's too small for a larger structure, on top of which the owner had died and the will was stuck in probate for months...."

He shrugged and tossed her a grin that was unabashedly smug. "As you said, I was lucky."

"How long ago was that?"

"About eight months now since the deal closed."

"Well, in that case no wonder you haven't—" Jenny broke off, aware that she might be creeping out on thin ice here. "What I mean to say is..."

"I know what you mean—there's still a lot of work to be done." He squeezed her hand and teased, "I was kind of hoping you'd volunteer your services..."

"Oh, David, do you mean it?" Jenny beamed at him like a kid at Christmas after Santa had granted a most favorite wish. "I just love doing this sort of thing."

"What—carpentry, painting?"

"All that stuff." Jenny was so excited about the prospect of actually being able to help turn David's lucky find into a showplace, she hardly noticed she'd been towed into the kitchen. She did note that David was holding her hand, and tried to hide her tingling reaction with chatter. "Don't you remember how I helped my Dad when he put that addition on our house?"

"Now that you mention it..."

Jenny tossed him a look. "I sure remember the way you'd be watching us, with that damn superior grin of yours."

"Really used to know how to push your buttons, didn't I, Jen?" David murmured. His eyes were on her hand in his, and he was thinking how delicate the bones in it were yet how strong and capable it felt. And, nestled in his, how good. He raised his eyes. Jenny was jolted by the fire in them. "What do I do these days to get a rise out of you?"

Jenny thought faintly that if a rise in temperature was what he was after, then all it apparently took was for David Waterman to look at her and hold her hand.

She managed a shaky laugh. "Calling me *babe* would probably do it."

"Well then." A glint of mischief lightened the unsettling intensity of his gaze. "How do you like your coffee, *babe?*"

And on her sharp inhalation of pretended umbrage, unmindful of the fact that he'd earlier berated himself for what he was about to do again, he kissed her full on the rounded O of her lips.

Before Jenny could recover sufficiently to do anything but stand there, David let go of her hand and stepped over to the counter. He tossed down the knife, filled a mug with coffee and held it out to her. "Cream and sugar?"

Meeting his innocent smile with a censuring look, Jenny took the cup from him. "No, thanks."

"Ready to eat?"

"Yes."

Afterward, replete from such tasty, and blessedly ordinary, breakfast fare as scrambled eggs, bacon and toast, David proudly showed Jenny the rest of his remodeled house. He had worked hard, she realized, having done a large share of the work himself in order to save money, but also, he told her, because he liked the idea of making a home for himself. A home that reflected who he was.

Jenny found that it certainly did that. He was a forward-thinking man, but apparently also a staunch traditionalist. The latest in gadgets and appliances lived hand in glove with some exquisite antiques. His choice of paintings, rugs, and his bedspread—bold colors, and even bolder shapes and designs—certainly reflected the outgoing, somewhat flamboyant side of him, just as his books and his vast and eclectic collection of records, tapes and discs told Jenny of a never-suspected deep-thinking, sensitive and even romantic side.

Some of this Jenny had either realized or suspected just by having been with him these past few weeks, but some of it—Nietzsche, Longfellow, the Brontës, Kant, rubbing up against books by Sheldon, Uris and Louis L'Amour—was a revelation.

All of it thrilled her.

His bedroom, on the other hand, very much distressed her. Not because it wasn't beautiful or cozy or inviting, but because it *was*. A wall had been knocked out to make the house's original two bedrooms into one large one. Just as in the living room, the wall facing the lake was all glass. Add to that a large skylight right above a king-size bed, a floor-to-ceiling fireplace and an inch-thick rug, and you had, in Jenny's opinion, a place designed for long nights of pleasure. The loving kind.

Something unpleasant shivered through her as she fleetingly wondered with whom David had last shared those pleasures in this room. Suddenly she couldn't get out of it fast enough.

David, ignorant of the wayward direction Jenny's thoughts had taken, followed more sedately. "I think a deck outside both the living- and bedroom, and a hot tub out there'd really add something, don't you?"

Boy, did she. "Hmm."

"It'll be my next project, if you care to sign up."

Only for work, no doubt, Jenny thought sourly, while someone else signed up to share the hot tub. "Hmm."

"Something wrong?"

"Wrong?"

David's odd, puzzled look made Jenny realize how strange her attitude must seem to him. She flushed with chagrin. "No, of course not," she hastened to assure him. "I was just...thinking."

"About what?"

"Oh," Jenny hedged, "relationships." Partially true, in any case. "How we tend to think we've got people all figured out only to realize..." she shrugged, giving a self-conscious little laugh "...we don't."

"Meaning?"

"Meaning I never figured you for a home owner, I guess," she evaded with another half-truth. "Or thought you'd become so domesticated."

She laced her fingers behind her back and sauntered out into the yard. "Next you'll be putting up a white picket fence and producing the requisite two-point-five offspring with some lucky little woman...."

She had meant to merely make a lighthearted crack, but once the words were out she was appalled by how wistful they sounded.

David's responding chuckle had a husky edge to it. He stepped up behind Jenny and gently turned her to face him. "And would you be interested in becoming someone's lucky little woman, Storky?"

"Heavens, no!" Jenny's quick and horrified denial was genuine enough. What dismayed her was that she made it not so much in response to David's softly voiced question, but because her first reaction had been to say, Yes— yours! She disengaged herself from his light hold. "And I warn you, the term *little woman* is another one that's guaranteed to get an instant rise out of me."

"You used it first."

"I was being facetious."

"So was I."

To hide an unexpected stab of disappointment, Jenny walked over to the canvas-covered car. "What's this?"

"A 1968 Corvette." David whipped off the tarpaulin, exposing a truly beautiful automobile, snow-white and gleaming. "And, thanks to all my hard work, pretty much in mint condition."

"Wow." Jenny was thoroughly impressed.

"You were expecting maybe a clunker?"

"Well..." Discomfited because his teasing tone now had a decided edge to it, Jenny gave a guilty little laugh. "Yeah." Catching his sardonic expression, she added defensively, "With your record, can you blame me?"

"It keeps cropping up with you, doesn't it?" he asked quietly, setting about putting the cover back on the car. "It keeps getting in the way."

"What does?"

"My record. How I used to be, what you thought I was."

"No, it doesn't."

"Doesn't it?" David demanded angrily. He slapped a palm against the car. "Can you honestly say you're not surprised this isn't a piece of junk? Or that what you saw inside the house isn't anything like you expected it to be?" He made a sound of disgust. "I wish you'd get it through your head that I'm not just a dumb jock anymore—"

"I never thought—"

"Didn't you?" Hands gripping her shoulders, David's gaze drilled into hers. "Didn't you really? Don't you still?"

"No." Helpless and dismayed in the face of his intensity, Jenny shook her head. "What can I say to you?"

"That you appreciate what I've done here. That you understand why it's important for me to be someone, have something. That you see how far I've come. And that you care."

He abruptly released her. Turning aside, he rubbed a hand across his mouth as if to erase what he'd just blurted out. He stared at the lake.

"Nobody ever expected me to make anything of myself," he said quietly, after a long silence Jenny hadn't known how to break. "Not even my folks. I went to college in spite of them. Old man Slater, the guy Russ and I worked for, paid for part of my tuition, and I scraped and scrambled and hustled for athletic scholarships to make up the rest. I scrounged meals and a pat on the head from the Daltons. After my parents divorced and we all went our separate ways, Bea and Frank Dalton were the ones I counted on, the ones who cared. Everybody else thought I was just a troublemaker, a loudmouthed jerk...."

He slanted Jenny a somber glance. "You want to know something funny, Stork?"

Jenny just looked at him in silent misery.

"There's only four people I've ever wanted to impress. The Daltons, Carl Slater and ... you."

"Oh, David." She mouthed the words but couldn't get a sound past the constriction in her throat. And when, after long moments of silent and mutual contemplation, David finally turned and walked away, Jenny didn't follow.

She headed for her car, instead.

Next morning, David arrived at Jenny's office just seconds after she did. One look at his face convinced her that he hadn't been any happier with the conclusion of their brunch date than she'd been. He launched into an apology without preamble.

"I'm sorry for the way I turned on you yesterday," he said, frowning down at her seated behind her desk. "I don't know what got into me."

"I do." Jenny got up off her chair and went to him. "Chicken livers."

He looked at her as if she'd lost her mind, and Jenny laughed. "Oh, David," she exclaimed, taking his arm and giving it a little shake, "don't you see? We're both stuck in some sort of time warp when it comes to each other. We both have misconceptions that stem from the way things used to be between us."

She released his sleeve and took a few steps away from him before turning to face him again. "I never thought you were a dumb jock, you know. Arrogant, obnoxious, generally insufferable? Oh yes, that I thought. But dumb? Never."

David studied her in silence for a moment, then gave a small nod of acceptance. A tiny smile tugged one side of his mouth upward while his brow crinkled in consternation. "All right, but . . . *chicken livers?*"

Impulsively Jenny rushed over and hugged him. "Just my way of reminding you that I'm no more a snooty egghead than you're a dumb jock. Can we agree to bury the past, do you think?"

Chapter Seven

Midweek they went to see a movie. An action flick Jenny really hadn't wanted to see but which she found surprisingly well acted and entertaining.

True to their agreement to bury the past, neither alluded to the fact that in the used-to-be time of their youth David wouldn't have dreamed of inviting Jenny to a picture like that, and Jenny wouldn't have accepted if he had.

Because they'd gone to an early show and it wasn't dark yet when they got out, they picked up hamburgers and shakes at a nearby fast-food drive-through to have as a picnic.

"I know a great spot to park up on Cougar Mountain," David said, and Jenny hoped it wasn't too serious an infringement of the rules of their pact when in response to David's statement she wryly thought, *I'll bet*. In any case, his grin showed he knew exactly what she'd been thinking.

He reached over to give her nose an affectionate little tweak. "When you see the view, you'll know the reason I've always liked it up there."

Right.

Smiling to herself, languid with undefined, dreamy contentment, Jenny leaned her head against the soft leather of the Corvette's bucket seat and closed her eyes. With the windows down, the breeze fanning her unbound hair and cooling her skin was fragrant with early summer. Freshly cut grass, the piney scent of sun-warmed conifers and the varied bouquets of flowers in bloom mingled with the earthier smells of horses and other animals in the paddocks and pastures they drove past.

Something mellow and soothing was playing on the radio. New-age or classical, it was hard to tell. Jenny found she didn't care about whatever kind of music it was any more than she cared where David was taking her. With luck, she mused with uncharacteristic whimsy, it'd be to some deserted island. It'd be kind of nice for a change not to have a business to worry about; no goals, no conflicts to complicate life, past, present and future. Just a bit of coconut and mango gathering, with maybe a fish or two to spear for protein.

Jenny chuckled. With her luck there'd be snakes—yards long and deadly.

"What's funny?" David jammed the stick shift into Park. He turned the key and killed the engine.

"Serpents in paradise," Jenny said, opening her eyes and laughing aloud at the face he pulled in response. "Just a bit of nonsense." Sitting up, she looked around. "Where is this?"

"On top of the world, I like to think. Look ahead." Pointing with his chin, he busied himself with the food. "I'm starved."

"Wow." Jenny had caught the view. Straight ahead, beyond the wooded hills dotted with houses, beyond the sparkling waters of the lake and the cloverleafs of interstate On and Off ramps, Seattle was just starting to turn on its lights.

In the gathering dusk it was like watching a Christmas tree being lit, candle by incandescent candle. It was magic. It was beautiful.

"Oh, David." Aware that he had a knack for reducing her to these simpering exclamations again and again yet unable to come up with anything more profound to express her emotions, Jenny turned to bestow a glowing smile of appreciation on him.

She caught him watching her almost anxiously, as if he'd been afraid she might not share his enthusiasm for the place.

"It's beautiful," she breathed.

"Told ya." He took a huge bite of his hamburger and made a show of happily chewing.

But Jenny knew him a little better by now and so could discern the relief and gratification he took such pains to hide.

They gazed out over the view in silence for a while. Around them darkness fell. They were enclosed inside the cab of the car as if in a capsule deep in outer space somewhere. Alone but not lonely. Warm. And before them the city's glittering lights like a sea of shining stars.

"So will you come to my house again on Sunday?" David asked at length.

"Do you want me to?"

"Would I ask if I didn't?"

Jenny chuckled. "I s'pose not. Should I be wearing my trusty carpenter apron?"

"You really got one of those?" Dave sounded impressed.

"Yep."

"By all means then, wear it." There was a pause, and then he said, deadpan, "Of course, I thought we'd go fishing, so shorts or a swimsuit might be more appropriate."

"Oh, you!" Jenny punched his arm.

"So do you like to fish?"

He shifted to face her then. In the murky darkness, Jenny could just about make out his features. They looked as mellow as his voice was sounding, and that pleased her.

"Sure I like to fish," she said.

"You got a rod?" He sounded skeptical.

"Yep."

"But can you catch anything with it?" *Blatant* skepticism.

"Can I catch—" Struck speechless with pretended outrage, Jenny stopped. She brought her face close to his. "I'll have you know, Mr. Waterman, that I am a Pisces. That means I'm a *fish*. And as such I not only swim like a fish, I think like a fish and I feel like a fish—"

"No, you don't." Dave trailed a finger down her arm, a touch Jenny forced herself to ignore.

"I can anticipate every movement a fish makes. You, sir—" she drew herself erect "—have before you the consummate fisherperson."

"Fisherperson." David covered his eyes in mock pain. "Spoken like a true woman of the nineties." He squinted at her through spread fingers. "We have something else in common, I see."

"Really?" Jenny tried to outguess this latest twist of his mind but couldn't. "Tell me."

"I, Ms. Jones, am a Pisces, too." He lowered his hand, sounding triumphant. "So what d'you think of that?"

Georgette was right, was what Jenny was thinking. Aloud she said, "Oh, brother," and closed her eyes.

"What's the matter?"

"We're both Pisces."

"I just said that."

"I know."

At Jenny's gloomy tone, David leaned over and lifted one of her eyelids so she'd look at him. "Something wrong with that?"

Jenny opened her other eye. "According to Georgette, that's why we fight."

"You discussed me—us—with Georgette Myerson?"

Thrown off balance by this indignant digression, Jenny blinked and automatically protested, "There is no 'us.'"

And got even more shook up when he countered, "Isn't there?"

"This dock was the first thing I rebuilt after I bought the house," David told Jenny as he stowed their fishing gear, as well as a cooler full of cold drinks, in his little runabout. "Didn't even wait for spring. I mean, what good is a house on the lake without a dock and a boat, right?"

"Right."

"So how do you like her?"

Jenny took the hand he held out to her and stepped aboard. "What, the boat or the dock?"

He shot her a look. "The boat, of course. A dock's not a 'her.'"

"But a boat is?"

"Sure. Put this on."

When he handed her a life jacket, Jenny protested. "Hey, I don't need that."

"You do on my boat, kiddo."

"I'm a fish, remember," Jenny grumbled, but she obediently slipped the lightweight orange vest on over her white tank top, regardless. "Swimming's second nature to me."

"Drowning would be first nature if you got bumped on the head and knocked unconscious."

"So how come Sly doesn't have to wear one?" Jenny nodded toward the cat curled up on one of the seats.

Dave yanked the cord to start the outboard engine and ignored her half-serious grousing.

Jenny sat down. "And what makes a boat female?"

Sweating and panting from his so-far fruitless attempts to start the motor, David straightened. "Anything with an engine *has* to be female." He bent to his task again, pulling once, twice. "Contrary as hell."

The engine roared to life. The arch look he tossed Jenny as he ducked next to her under the canopy shading the two front seats of the boat plainly said, see?

Jenny decided to let it pass.

As David skillfully backed the boat away from the dock before executing a sleek turn and pouring on the gas, she watched Sly surefootedly negotiate his way along the side of the boat to the bow. Once there, she was astounded to see him sit himself down and commence to stare frontward. His moth-eaten ears flapping in the warm breeze, his fur ruffling, he sat unmoving like a ship's ornament.

"I always thought cats hated water," she remarked.

"They do, and so does Sly," David replied, cutting power to idle so they could troll as they fished. "But he loves boats."

"How long have you had him?"

"He sort of came with the house." He said it gruffly, frowning, as he stared straight ahead. "My folks never let me have a pet, but there he was. It seemed like fate."

Jenny nodded. She understood about fate, strongly believed in it, herself. It was that belief, in fact, that had helped her so much in accepting Russell's death. And, once she'd weathered the first shock of her loss, it had helped her in not assigning the blame for the accident to David.

"Why 'Sly'?" she asked.

David chuckled then, turning toward her. "It's short for Sylvester."

"Oh." It fit, she thought. The cat was obviously a fighter, if his battered appearance was anything to go by, and David had always been a big *Rocky* fan. "As in Stallone, right?"

"Wrong. Jeez, Stork." Visibly disgusted with her, David got up and, crouching until he'd cleared the canopy, moved to the back to busy himself with his rod.

Jenny stared after him, nonplussed. "Now what did I say?"

David glowered. "Your preconceptions are showing again."

"What?"

"There's other Sylvesters, you know, as in, 'I tink I taw a putty-tat!'"

Jenny's jaw dropped and, for a long moment she could only stare. He looked so gorgeously ludicrous, standing with his hands on his narrow hips clad in the skimpiest of swim trunks, tanned muscular legs spread apart for balance in the gently rocking boat, and his face indignant while doing that preposterous imitation.

And then she howled. "That's the funniest thing I ever saw," she gasped.

David's expression turned sheepish. He actually blushed, making Jenny break up all over again.

"Yeah, well," he grumbled. "That's the Sylvester Sly's named for."

Jenny sat on the floor of the boat and, shaking her head, squinted up at him. "You never cease to amaze me," she said slowly, and had to clear her throat because something in it suddenly made her voice catch. She was flooded with the oddest feelings, too, and it took all of her self-control not to reach out and fiercely hug him.

David too was struggling for control over his emotions. He felt foolish now where moments ago he'd felt hurt and angry, and not long before that, self-conscious about having adopted a cat and as much as admitting he'd always wanted a pet.

He could remember ridiculing Jenny's obvious attachment to the scruffy little pooch she used to have, and Russell's penchant for gerbils and guinea pigs. Of course, he'd known the reason he gave them a rough time about their animals was because he so badly wished he had one of his own, but he'd never wanted them to know that. Now Jenny probably did.

How was it he, who'd always prided himself on his ability to fool people into thinking that he was obnoxious, arrogant and uncaring...how was it that these days he was making such a career of laying himself bare to Storky Jones, of all people?

Look at her, he told himself disgustedly with a quick glance at her averted face, the poor woman can't even meet your eyes. You're making her uncomfortable as hell.

"Hey." He forced a light tone and extended a hand to help Jenny up. "What say we do what we came here to do, fish."

Accepting his hand and scrambling awkwardly to her feet, Jenny tossed him a wry, sideways smile. "If that's your new name for me, I'm not sure I like it."

He chuckled, glad to have her teasing him again, and handed her the rod. "Need help putting on bait?"

"Nope."

Pretty good, he thought, watching her deftly accomplish the task. "Do you want port or starboard to fish from?"

"I'll take starboard..." she tossed her baited hook into the water and slanted him a twinkling look as she reeled out more line "...since it's in keeping with my political views."

David groaned. "An elephant, wouldn't you know it."

"Beats being a donkey."

They grinned at each other, then settled down to do some serious trolling in companionable silence.

"So are you really Republican?" David asked idly after a while. Neither of them had had as much as a bite and they were drowsing in their seats at the back of the boat, their rods stuck in the holders at the side.

"Hmm." Jenny lazily stretched her bare legs into the aisle, giving David a most advantageous view of their shapely lengths. "I usually tend to vote issues rather than straight party tickets."

"So do I."

"Well." She opened one eye and smiled at him. "I guess that's something else we've got in common, then, isn't it?"

"I guess." Their gazes and smiles lingered on each other in mutual appreciation.

And then David snapped upright. "You've got a bite!"

"What?" Jenny was slower to react.

"A bite, a bite." Dave was on his feet and at her rod, hurriedly working to tug it out of the holder. "Damn, but he's a fighter."

"What're you doing!?" Jenny was on her feet, too. "Gimme my rod!" She shouldered into him, tried to take it from him.

"Don't!" Flushed with excitement, frantically reeling the line in and out to give the fish enough freedom to wear itself out—it had to be a salmon, ten pounds at least!—David was not about to give up the rod.

"What do you mean, *don't*?" Jenny shouted, reaching across him, shoving him. "That's my fish, dammit. Give it to me!"

She lunged, he tried to sidestep, ward her off. He tripped, teetered and, with the fish deciding at that moment to swim for its life, toppled. Arms flailing, his body responded to the mighty yank on the line from the fleeing fish with a sharp forward motion and, with Jenny still screeching and wildly grappling for the pole, overboard he went.

In a sideways, graceless little dive, so did Jenny.

They both shot to the surface, spluttering and treading water, within a foot of each other—just in time to see Jenny's rod whiz out of sight at a rapid clip.

"See what you made me do!"

"Well, I hope you're satisfied!"

They yelled at each other in unison, glaring as best they could with water streaming from and into their eyes. Blinking, swiping at their faces with dripping hands, their blazing gazes met and, simultaneously struck by the hilarity of the situation, crinkled.

"If you could've seen yourself..."

"The expression on your face when..."

Laughing, slapping their hands on the water like frolicking otters, they lay back and let their life jackets carry them.

"The boat!" David struggled upright; Jenny quickly followed. And then they both broke up again.

The boat was slowly drifting away from them, which, while not exactly a laughing matter, was no great calamity, either, since there wasn't another boat in sight anywhere and they were still within easy swimming distance of both the boat and shore. No, what was funny was Sly, the cat.

With the kind of total unperturbability only a feline was able to exhibit, he sat on the bow as regal as ever, daintily licking his paw and washing his face.

"Now that's what I call poise," Jenny exclaimed with heartfelt envy, only to be contradicted by David.

"Uh-uh," he said, setting out after the boat with a leisurely breaststroke. "That's cool, man. Real *cool*."

Despite the relatively warm day, they were both shivering by the time they tied up at the dock. They hadn't thought to bring towels, so Jenny's hair hung in wet hanks down her back and across her shoulders. David's was slicked back and close to his head in a way that sharply accentuated his cheekbones and gave him a hawklike and predatory look that Jenny found decidedly disturbing.

Once docked, they chucked off their life jackets and stowed them under the seats. David lithely jumped ashore, then turned to give Jenny a hand just as she straightened and faced him.

His mouth went dry. His mind went blank except for one very carnal thought. Half-bent, his hand still stretched toward her, he devoured her with his eyes.

Standing as she did, tall and straight, she seemed to him like Aphrodite, risen from the sea. Her legs, sun kissed and endless, sprang from slim, shapely hips clad in the briefest of pale blue shorts. A white tank top, its thin cotton rendered practically transparent, clung wetly to her torso. It showed off a tiny waist, while leaving nothing about her full breasts and puckered nipples to David's imagination.

He drank in their riveting sight, the proud thrust, the tempting swell of them. Like a man dying of thirst in the desert who's finally been offered a drink, he moistened his lips with his tongue—and raised his eyes to Jenny's.

They were wide pools of sapphire, huge, and...aware.

The realization fanned his flickering desire into a raging wildfire of need. Staring into her eyes, he saw the corresponding hunger and was lost.

She offered her hand and, catching it in his, David hauled her off the boat and against him there on the dock. With his gaze unblinkingly riveted to hers, giving her time to fully understand his intentions, they stood belly to belly for a long, pulsing moment.

And then, with a groan, David drew her face toward his and cut off any belated objections with the hot possession of his kiss. His mouth, open and demanding, covered hers, slanting and probing until Jenny's lips conformed to his. The hand on her chin slid around to grip the back of her head, fingers splayed. His free arms enclosed and brought her body flush against his.

At the very first contact of their bodies, Jenny's senses had exploded in a frenzy of desire. Briefly she teetered on the brink of rational thought, and then David's tongue touched hers. Thinking stopped, and she gave herself up to simply feeling.

On fire, she eagerly welcomed the onslaught of his tongue and teeth, kissing him back with an abandon she had never felt before. Unable to do otherwise, she wound both arms around his middle, holding him as tightly as he was holding her. Every nerve in her body yearned for the ultimate closeness.

How solid he felt. He was like an anchor in the sea of mindless passion in which she was adrift. How good he smelled—his scent was of man, of fresh air and of the lake they'd just been dunked in, and was at once a comfort and a titillation. Burying her nose in the warmth of his neck, Jenny breathed of him deeply, then lifted her lips for another soul-shattering kiss.

Gradually, the terrible thirst for her blunted but far from slaked, David was able to lessen the pressure of his mouth and let it grow tender.

"Jenny," he rasped, "my beautiful, beautiful Jenny..." Gently now his tongue courted hers. His lips stroked and caressed the satin-slick heat of hers, absorbed their arousing tremor and caught them fiercely once again.

Feverish with rebounding need, he feasted on her like a starving man. He wanted nothing so much as to lay her down and make her his completely. Right then. Right there. But some shred of sanity tempered his clamoring passion and reminded him of where they were.

Not fifty feet from them in either direction, his neighbors' docks jutted out into the lake, and the mostly glass walls of their houses were like so many eyes watching them.

And so he pulled back, little by little, nuzzling and teasing with tongue and teeth, trailing small kisses across Jenny's face, her eyes, giving her time to collect her wits just as he was trying to collect his.

When at last she lifted her lids and met his gaze with a mixture of vulnerability, defensiveness and lingering hunger, he had himself sufficiently in hand to muster a cocky grin.

Leaning close, he dropped a final kiss onto the tip of her nose. "I briefly considered steaming up the neighbors' windows right here and now," he murmured, "but then I decided to leave that for another time." His eyes searched hers. "I want to make love with you, Jenny."

Swallowing, her gaze steady on his, Jenny almost imperceptibly nodded.

"Now, Jen. As soon as we're inside."

Again she nodded. "Yes."

The word was a sigh that David swallowed with the fiery possession of his kiss. Jenny gave herself up to it. And when he tore his lips from hers, swung her effortlessly up in his arms and set off with her toward the house, she buried her face in the crook of his neck with a sigh of blissful anticipation.

She didn't lift her head until she felt David come to an jarring stop with a short Anglo-Saxon expletive her mother would have washed David's mouth out with soap for using. She almost used it herself, however, when she followed his gaze and saw what he saw.

The Daltons. Just scrambling out of their car, Bea with a gleam in her eye and a casserole dish in her hands. Frank, giving them a quick once-over, held a cake carrier and smiled an embarrassed apology.

"Surprise!" Bea shouted gaily.

"I'll say." This from David, for Jenny's ears only.

She stifled a giggle. "Please put me down."

Reluctantly he did.

"You two been swimming?" Beatrice asked.

"Fishing," said David.

"And then we fell in," Jenny felt compelled to add.

"Best get out of those wet things then, the two of you," Bea said, beaming. "Or you'll catch your death. Frank and I'll get dinner."

"Dinner!" Jenny and David exclaimed in unison.

"Of course, dinner," Bea, looking angelically innocent, tossed back blithely, already walking into the house. "After all, we came to celebrate Davey's birthday."

Jenny's bewildered gaze flew to David. "It's your birthday?"

He thought. "Is today the twenty-seventh?"

"I think so."

"Of February?"

"Uh-uh. Of June."

"Well, then it can't be my birthday, can it?"

Jenny grimaced. "Maybe you should mention that little fact to Bea."

"She won't care." He looked so pained, so much like a kid whose favorite cookie's been snatched from his hand and devoured by the family dog, that Jenny forgot her own crushing disappointment and burst out laughing. It struck her that she'd laughed more during her short time with David than she had in years.

"You're right," she said, "she won't." Catching his face between both of her hands, she pressed a kiss onto each pulled-down corner of his mouth. "Happy *Un*birthday, *Davey*." She released him before he could respond, calling back as she sprinted toward the house, "Race you to the shower."

Even with her head start, he easily beat her but let her use his bathroom first, anyway.

"Put this on," he said, handing her a short kimono-style, terry-cloth robe, "and toss your things out. I'll stick 'em in the dryer."

Warm from her shower, as well as from the feel and smell of David's robe, Jenny found Beatrice happily fussing in the kitchen with Frank looking on.

"You can do a salad," she was told. "I brought a shrimp casserole, and Davey said there's rolls in the freezer. Frank made the cake."

"Really, Pop? I love your cakes." Jenny kissed Frank's cheek. "Hi," she said in belated greeting.

"Hi, yourself." He gave her a quick squeeze, looking uncomfortable. "Look, if we're interrupting—"

"We're not, are we, Jenny?" said Bea, arms akimbo. "We always come for Davey's birthday."

"Yes, but in February, dear." This, quietly from Frank, but if he meant to burst Bea's bubble, he failed.

"I know that!" she exclaimed indignantly. "But the boy was out of town then, wasn't he? And afterward it got forgotten. Until now."

"But Jenny's here...."

"Good." Bea bent to check the oven. "About time he had someone besides us to celebrate with."

"Didn't his Mom ever come?" Jenny asked, frowning.

"Not since she got married again and moved to Chicago. She's had two more kids, you know. Girls."

Jenny absently watched Bea rummage in a drawer, then slam it shut without taking anything out. She wondered how David felt about having two little sisters. She'd always wanted siblings, herself, but her mother hadn't been able to have more children. And she'd had Russell, of course, to grow up and share with. Who had David had?

"What about his father?" Fathers and sons often shared a special bond, Jenny knew, because Frank and Russell certainly had. And though David had already hinted that this hadn't been so in his case, she longed to hear otherwise from an outside source.

"John David?" Bea's look spoke volumes of contempt. "Married a gal younger than his son, last I heard, and living in Los Angeles." She bestowed a fond glance on her husband. "Frank here was more of a father to David than that man ever was."

"Now, Bea," Frank chided, carefully putting candles on the birthday cake, "we hardly knew the man."

"And neither did David," Bea concluded acerbically.

"Did I hear my name?" Dressed in jeans and a UW Huskies sweatshirt, his feet bare, David sauntered into the kitchen. He sniffed. "Something sure smells good."

"It'll taste even better." Bea's smile held a world of affection. "If you'll pour us some wine and take Frank out from under our feet, maybe Jenny and I can see about getting it on the table."

"Aye, aye, sir."

"Watch it, boy," Bea blustered. "You're not too old to spank."

He caught her around the waist and, kissing her cheek, winked at Jenny. "I love you, too, hon."

"Isn't he awful?" Bea giggled like a girl, and Jenny wanted to hug David for making her so happy.

"Terrible," she said past the lump forming in her throat.

Despite their initial, horrified reaction to seeing the Daltons in David's driveway, dinner had been a lively, fun-filled affair for both Jenny and David. They'd insisted on doing the dishes alone, however, and for once Frank had prevailed in hustling Beatrice out of there and into their car.

So now Jenny and David leaned back against the closed front door and rolled their heads sideways to give each other smiling but rueful looks.

"Phew," they went in unison, then chuckled.

"It was lovely, though, wasn't it?" Jenny said.

"Wonderful." David's smile turned wicked. "The only way it could've been better, is if they hadn't come."

"Oh, David." Jenny, though inwardly concurring, punched his arm. "You're terrible."

He twisted toward her then, his expression grave. "The only thing that's terrible," he said softly, "is that now we've had time to do some thinking."

"We have?" Jenny asked in a small voice, feeling a clutch of disappointment even though she, too, had entertained moments of second thoughts.

"Hmm." He reached out and with one finger traced the smooth contour of her cheek. "The step we were about to take before Bea and Pop showed up was pretty irrevocable."

Jenny, quivering beneath his gentle caress, nodded. "I know."

"Something important is happening between us, Jen," David said, adding the rest of his hand to his touch, cupping her cheek. "Something beyond friendship. Something we might want to think about carefully before rushing into."

They gazed at each other in silence, and some of what they'd felt earlier rekindled. In response to the feeling, David leaned over and kissed Jenny. Except this time he kept his passion tightly leashed. Even when Jenny turned into him and wound her arms around his neck, even when her lips softened and opened beneath the pressure of his, he held himself back.

A part of Jenny, the sane part, appreciated and applauded David's restraint. Yet, another part, the Eve part, the part that had tempted as long as men and women had been on earth, wanted to break his restraint and make him mad for her. As mad for her as he had been earlier, and as she was for him even now.

To what end, though? Try as she might, Jenny couldn't quite still that niggling question.

She eased her grip on him, made herself firm her lips in a series of withdrawing pecks. "I agree," she said, and smiled to show that it didn't kill her to say so.

"Right."

Altruism sure wasn't what it was cracked up to be, David thought, hurting like a teenager with unfulfilled desire as he slowly let Jenny go. "We ought to at least sleep on it," he said. Catching a wry glance from her, he quickly added, "Alone, I mean."

"I knew what you meant." Jenny let her gaze mesh with his and was warmed and reassured by the heat. "So how do we proceed?"

"With caution, I think." They both laughed, a little giddily, their gazes unable to let go.

"Next weekend's the Fourth of July," David said. "A friend of mine has a cabin on Orcas he lets me use...."

"Won't he want it?" Jenny asked, her heartbeat speeding up at the prospect of four whole days together with David.

"He's in Europe, and I've got the key."

"Oh."

"Is it a date?" Hauling her close, David kissed her.

It was quite a while before Jenny could answer, and by then, as breathless and tempted as he, she was running out to her car as fast as her feet would carry her. "Yes!"

She drove home more or less on automatic pilot, her thoughts turned inward, questioning, searching. Undeniably, some extremely compelling force was at work between herself and David Waterman.

Looking back, she supposed he had always had a sort of dark fascination for her. On some not to be too closely examined level, he had always drawn her. He'd been temptation in the way that wet paint seemed like an irresistible temptation to touch, or the way the copy of *Lady Chatterley's Lover* had called out to her from her mother's bookshelf after someone had told her about the spicy parts.

The difference was, Jenny realized, that while she had inevitably succumbed to those other temptations—she'd touched the paint and read the book—she'd always fought tooth and nail against David Waterman. She'd told herself she didn't want any part of him when—she knew that now—the truth was the only reason she hadn't wanted him was that she'd known she couldn't have him. Hadn't he daily made it clear he had no use for her?

Just like he daily made clear he had no use for pets.

"Oh, Lord." Jenny groaned aloud.

Pretense, that's what the bulk of their nonrelationship had consisted of right up until the moment she'd bid on him at the auction. That night, for one mad moment, she'd gone beyond it, only to instantly retreat. Except it had been too late. The die had been cast, and from then on, slowly, inexorably, they'd been forced to strip away the pretense and begin the move toward understanding each other.

Understanding each other and—*having* each other.

It was the latter that was giving Jenny headaches as she got ready to crawl into her solitary bed that night. Removing and folding the bedspread, she thought, In just five more nights my sleep won't be solitary anymore. She shuddered with a mixture of anticipation and dread.

Caution, reserve, was very much a part of Jenny's nature. Not for her those impetuous leaps into the sack with any likely candidate as so many of her peers seemed comfortable doing. Other than the pathetically few times with Russell, she'd been intimate with only two other men, and even then not until she'd known them for a good, long time. The encounters had been pleasant, but not earth-shaking, and when the affairs ended, there'd always been an element of relief mixed in with the inevitable regret about losing a friend.

The thing that had her quaking, now that she was no longer in David's intoxicating presence and her blood had cooled, was not the fear, the *certainty,* that to have an affair with David would change her forever. No, it was more than that. Much more.

Chapter Eight

She had fallen in love with David Waterman.

The realization didn't give Jenny any more peace come the light of day than it had when it hit her in the dead of night. What it did do was give her considerable pause about the course of action to which she had agreed while blinded by passion.

True, David was no longer the randy Don Juan he'd been when he was younger. *Or so he claimed.*

Pounding the pavement on the punishing morning run she'd hoped would help get things into perspective, Jenny made herself dismiss the intrusive thought. No use clouding the issue further with nebulous doubts, she told herself sternly, because, Don Juan or not, it seemed unlikely he intended to live happily ever after with her.

Something important is happening between us, Jen. Something beyond friendship.

David had said that last night, and at the time, her senses inflamed and clamoring, the words had sounded full of promises.

But, on sober reflection, Jenny realized that nothing whatever in his words or demeanor, either before or after that one declaration, had indicated anything but rampant lust on his part. Lust that was no doubt partially fueled by a genuine affection for her, but, surely, equally by the fact that she'd seemed unattainable during all those years of their youth.

To finally have a secret desire about to be fulfilled was a powerful aphrodisiac, as Jenny herself could attest. Except that in her case, love had crept in to complicate things. So much so, that she knew their stolen weekend on Orcas would be, for her, a huge mistake. To be loved—in the physical sense—and then left by David Waterman would be more than she could bear, now that she knew her heart was involved. Much better to keep things between them as they were, platonic. She wouldn't go with David to Orcas, and she would tell him immediately, before he made any further plans.

He wouldn't like her backing out, and there was no way she could tell him the reason she was doing so. He'd be disappointed, probably even angry. He might not want to see her at all after this, but even that would be better than to have her heart broken a few weeks or months down the line.

Jenny called David's apartment the minute she came home from her run. All she got was his answering machine, so she showered and drove to her office before calling him from there.

"I'm sorry, Mr. Waterman is out of town until tomorrow evening. Could someone else help you, or would you care to leave a message?"

The latter was tempting but cowardly. "No, thank you." Jenny hesitated. "This is Eugenie Jones. By any chance did Mr. Waterman leave a message for me?"

"Just a moment while I check."

Jenny waited. While they hadn't spoken of getting together before the Fourth, David hadn't mentioned a trip out of town, either. On the other hand, why should he have felt the need to?

"Ms. Jones?"

"Yes?"

"There's no message, but I spoke with Mr. Kastell, the senior pilot, and he said to tell you Mr. Waterman is flying an unexpected charter."

"Oh, I see. Thank you."

Breaking the connection, Jenny chewed her lip, thinking, Darn it, anyway. She'd been primed to tell him she'd changed her mind and had been ready to field whatever arguments he was bound to offer. And now this.

She picked up the ghastly German novel she'd been plodding away on and instantly tossed it down again. No way would she be able to concentrate on the thing until her talk with David was out of the way.

Complications. With a groan, she let her forehead drop onto her arms, folded on top of her desk. Oh, Lord, she thought with despair, these were exactly the kinds of emotional complications she'd always run from like the wind.

David hadn't done any charter flights in years and wouldn't have flown this one if he'd had a choice. His time was much better spent these days managing the business and selling its services. Yet when the call from a good corporate client came in and all of his other pilots were already booked—well, he had no choice but to take care of the job.

Truth to tell, he was delighted to do it. He'd flown the route up the coast of British Columbia to the Queen Charlottes in this very floatplane more times than he cared to remember, but the scenery was spectacular and he never tired of looking down at it. Besides, the return trip would be solo, since the corporate types and their two Japanese visitors were staying in their fisherman's paradise clear through the holiday weekend, so he'd have plenty of time to think of his own plans with Jenny Jones.

Storky.

He knew he had it bad when just thinking of her had the blood pounding in his veins. Very bad.

Damn, but it felt good.

Recalling that he had four passengers for whose safety and comfort he was responsible, David forced his thoughts to remain in the here and now. Time enough on the return flight tomorrow for dreams and introspection.

He pointed to a small island, little more than a rocky outcrop, on which hundreds of seals were sunning themselves. He banked sharply and circled down to give his passengers a closer look, as well as to allow the foreign visitors to take pictures.

Flying charters in a six-seater, single-engine floatplane like the one they were in on this trip, required that the pilot be a combination flight attendant and tour guide, as well. After passing Customs and refueling in Campbell River, B.C., David handed back thermoses of hot tea and coffee, as well as sandwiches, or harder stuff for those of his passengers who cared to imbibe.

His takeoff from Murdock Island the next morning was as faultless as his landing had been on arrival. The small bay in which he'd set down was as smooth as a millpond, and the tide had safely submerged the jagged rocks that might otherwise have tripped him up. His passengers were in good hands in the fishing camp below, the sky was a cloudless, azure dome, and the winds were calm. If he'd had one, David might have put the plane on automatic pilot and caught a nap, conditions were that great.

Except that sleep was the last thing on his mind, in any case.

Jenny was on his mind. And love was on his mind. The kind of love he planned to make to her and with her for one glorious, endless weekend. Slow love, hot love, delicious and naughty love.

He'd love her so hard, she'd be limp as a rag, and then he'd love her again. And again. He'd love her till every last bit of her stiff-necked reserve was reduced to jelly. Till she was putty in his hands. And then—

Here the salacious daydreams which were making David's blood race and his body grow tight abruptly came to an end. *And then* became a question, suddenly, instead of the lead-in into yet another lustful variation of his plans for Storky Jones and their coming long weekend.

Frowning, his string of heartfelt curses mercifully drowned out by the noisy drone of the small plane's engine, David glared into the vast, blue beyond and wondered where that irksome inner voice he heard had come from. The voice that, with a sneer, was asking him, *And then what?* And then you bring her to heel, you make her want, and hurt, as bad as you do? Is that it? Huh? Is it revenge you want? Getting even? Take her down a peg for all the times she's stuck her nose up in the air? Is that it, Waterman?

No! Upset, David jerked the stick. The plane bucked, its nose shot up. Airing another collection of colorful expletives, Dave brought it back on course. *No, dammit—it wasn't like that at all.*

A-ha! the voice—his conscience?—cackled triumphant-ly. So it's happily ever after you want with her. It's wedding bells, connubial bliss, the pitter-patter of—

Whoa! Just a cotton-pickin' minute there! The Cessna was bucking again, responding to the agitation of the man at her controls. *Wedding bells? Connubial bliss? With Storky Jones?*

Genuine amusement had him laughing aloud. Why, even if she'd have him—which there wasn't a snowball's chance in hell she would—they'd kill each other off before the honeymoon was even half over. They were too different, or maybe too much alike, whatever. They'd never make it work.

Would they?

For one crazy instant, David let himself imagine how it might be: It'd be intense, no doubt about that. It'd be interesting. It'd be irritating as hell. And insane. Definitely and certifiably *insane!*

He laughed again, a mite hollowly this time, and shook his head. He wanted Jenny; he liked her. Quite a lot, if truth be told. They sparked. She made him hot. He squirmed in his seat, loosened his collar. Boy, did she. She made him want to eat her alive, and—a slow smile replaced the remnants of a persistent frown—this weekend he'd make her want him in just the same way.

And then? That question again!

The frown snapped back in place. Impatient now to be out of the crate and away from the thoughts that plagued him, David poured on the power and headed the plane toward home.

And Jenny.

"Frankly, Bill, if I seem surprised it's only because I didn't think it would happen this soon."

Jenny lowered the left hand she'd held up in front of her to better admire the ring on her finger, and gave Bill Shafer a quick, happy smile, before her gaze returned to it. "I think it's magnificent."

Talk about understatement, she thought, all but blinded by the brilliance of the large ruby solitaire surrounded by six diamonds, each of which considerably exceeded the value of her own mother's half-carat engagement ring.

She drew it off her finger and handed it back to Bill. "Georgette will adore it."

"You think so?"

"I know so." Jenny leaned toward him on her office couch and pressed a kiss onto his cheek. "Congratulations, Bill. I couldn't be happier. When will you—"

The phone rang.

"Excuse me, would you?" Jenny rose and walked to her desk. "I told Ruth to hold my calls, so this had better be important. Yes, Ruth? All right, put her through. It's a friend of mine," she explained to Bill, covering the mouthpiece. "Bea! What's up? No, I don't have the radio on. No, as a matter of fact I'm standing, nor do I need to— *What?* When? Where? Oh, I see...."

Lowering the phone because her arm had suddenly lost its starch, Jenny turned toward Bill. She perceived more than saw that he was on his feet and looking at her with alarm, and heard as if from a distance, Bea's frantic voice issuing from the dangling phone.

"Jenny? Jenny are you there?"

"I-it's David," Jenny whispered, "he's..."

A roaring filled her ears, drowning out all other sound. The telephone dropped from her lifeless fingers. Her knees buckled. The room spun, its walls tilted. Clutching air, Jenny sank to the floor that rushed up to meet her.

* * *

She was lying on the couch in her office, Jenny realized with a small jolt of surprise. Ruth was chafing her hands, and she could hear Bill Shafer talking on the phone in a take-charge tone that she'd never heard him use before.

She opened her eyes, frowning. What on earth . . . ?

And then she remembered. David's plane had disappeared from the radar screen. Presumed to have crashed . . . no radio signal . . .

A searing stab of pain through her chest tore a keening moan from Jenny's lips, and she squeezed her eyes shut against a rush of scalding tears.

"Jenny." It was Ruth's voice, urgent, full of concern. "Jenny, look at me."

"D-David is . . . dead."

"Nonsense." Ruth's tone brooked no contradiction. "He is temporarily missing, but he's not dead. He's an experienced pilot, the weather couldn't be better. Jenny, do you hear me?"

But Jenny was beyond hearing just then. *Not David,* her mind screamed. *Please, not David. I beg you, God, don't let it be David. . . .*

"Jenny!" Someone was shaking her. "Jenny, for God's sake get a hold of yourself."

Blinking, her lids as heavy as if weights had been attached to her lashes, Jenny struggled to open her eyes and to get a hold of her galloping panic. David couldn't be the one who was dead. He was too vital, too alive. *Dear God, let it be—*

"Jenny!"

Jenny's eyes popped open, and she stared, aghast, at Ruth. Where was she? Where had she been? And what, sweet mercy, had she been thinking?

"Jenny, Mr. Shafer's been on the phone with Georgette's station ever since you—" Ruth stopped speaking and awkwardly stroked Jenny's cheek. "Ever since Mrs. Dalton called. They're out looking for him, honey. It'll be all right, you'll see."

Wearily Jenny nodded, even though she knew that, no matter what the outcome, for her nothing would ever be all right again. The knowledge caused her such physical pain that nausea roiled in her stomach like some noxious witches' brew.

She struggled upright, sure she'd be sick if she didn't get her head up off the pillow. "No, I'm okay," she assured Ruth, who was gently trying to press her back against the cushions. "I'm fine now, Ruth. Really."

And, indeed, she sounded fine. Composed, in charge of herself and her emotions, the way Rosalie Jones had taught her daughter to be and sound in front of others, no matter what. Jenny knew that, as it had in the past, this often-rebelled-against training would once again stand her in good stead. It would help her get through the rest of her life with her sanity intact.

Her legs felt unsteady when she first stood on them, but by taking a deep breath, locking her knees and stiffening her spine, she was able to overcome this remnant of her inner weakness. She walked carefully over to Bill Shafer, and only the closest observer would have seen by the rigid set of her shoulders and her tightly clenched fists how much this outward show of control was costing her.

Bill hung up the phone and turned to her. "According to the KXYZ newsroom," he said, "search boats are out looking for Waterman now." Taking Jenny's hand, he awkwardly patted it. "Everything will be fine, my dear, you'll see."

"Thank you." Jenny returned the squeeze of his hands and stretched tightly compressed lips into a semblance of a smile.

"They say he dropped off the radar screen due west of Anacortes," Bill said. "The area is thick with islands, Jenny, and, at this time of year, on a day as fine as today, small craft and fishing vessels are out in full force. They'll find him."

"Of course." She gently extracted her hand from his crushingly reassuring grip. "I think I'll drive out there."

"But—"

Both Ruth and Bill started to protest at once, but a sharp glance from Jenny silenced them. "Look," she told them, "I can't just sit around here and wait. Maybe there's something I can do out there...."

Anything, she thought, anything at all had to be better than to spend even one more emotion-laden moment in the company of these two well-meaning people.

Make that four well-meaning people.

Jenny closed her eyes and stifled a groan as Bea and Frank Dalton rushed into her office. "Darling, are you all right?"

Of all the people in the world, these two, at this time, were the very last ones Jenny could cope with. And so, after making a desperate lunge for her purse on the floor beside her desk, she mumbled an indistinct apology and shouldered past them out of the room.

In a futile hope of diverting her troubled thoughts with music, Jenny put a Beethoven tape into the tape player of her car, then proceeded to ignore the soothing music as she sped along I-405, and merged onto I-5. Soon she had left Seattle's northern bedroom communities, as well as the city of Everett behind, and the Skagit Valley lay spread before her, gilded by the almost setting sun.

The valley was fruitful and picturesque, framed by verdant hills. Snowcapped Mount Baker loomed in the distance.

Jenny saw but didn't absorb the beauty as she would have normally. She had closed herself off to everything, held every thought, every emotion at bay and would continue to do so until she knew that David was safe or…not.

She took the State Route 536 exit to Anacortes as if by rote; certainly she couldn't remember making a conscious decision. She hadn't been to Anacortes before, but it was as if some power outside of herself had taken over her wheels and so she got there with an unerring sense of direction.

She bypassed the town, the strip of motels and shops, and pulled to a stop at one of a seemingly myriad selection of marinas at just about the same time a seen-better-days fishing trawler tied up at the dock.

Jenny got out of her car but stayed next to it, her arms tightly wrapped around herself, watching as television news crews scrambled past her car for close-ups. An ambulance, its siren winding down to a discordant wail, squealed to a rocking stop in front of the gangplank leading down to the boat. In moments two medics with a stretcher were scrambling down it. An eternity later—so it seemed to Jenny, though it might only have been minutes—they made their way back up much more slowly.

Jenny craned her neck, the media focused their cameras and shouted rapid-fire questions at a cockily smiling but, from Jenny's vantage point at least, unhurt David Waterman.

Relief momentarily drained Jenny of strength, and she slumped against the side of her car. Releasing the breath she'd been unaware of holding, in one long, shuddering exhalation, she closed her eyes and gave a quick, heartfelt prayer of thanks.

"Hey, I'm fine, fellas," she could hear David call out to the press in passing. Then vehicle doors were being slammed, and Jenny opened her eyes just in time to see the ambulance slowly pull away from the dock.

She scrambled into her car, started the engine and set out after it. It wasn't far to the hospital, and she reached the place just moments after the aid unit had pulled up at the emergency entrance. But by the time she'd parked her car and hurried inside after them, David was nowhere in sight.

Spotting the nursing station, she walked over to inquire after him.

"He's in the treatment room," was all they could tell her, of course, since he'd only just arrived. Resigned to a lengthy wait, hospitals being what they were, Jenny sat down on one of the chairs lined up against one wall of the wide, overbright hallway. The medics, carrying their collapsed gurney, came out of one of the rooms and headed for the exit.

Jenny shot to her feet and hurried after them. "Excuse me," she called. "Please..."

One was already out the door, the other, older one, was holding it open with his rump while they waited for Jenny to catch up.

"Please," she repeated, a little breathlessly, "David Waterman—is...how is he?"

"You the wife?"

Jenny flushed. "F-fiancée," she stuttered, caught off guard by the question and afraid they might not tell her anything if she said she was just a friend.

"Been worried, have ya?"

"Yes." Jenny returned their kindly smiles with a shaky one of her own. "Is he all right?"

"Right as rain, pretty much. Lucky young cuss. A knot on the head, slight concussion, couple of banged up ribs is about the extent of it. Course the doc's checking him over, but I'm pretty sure he'll be fine."

Acknowledging Jenny's thanks with a friendly nod, they strode off. Through the glass doors Jenny watched them stow the stretcher, then climb into the cab. The flashing lights were turned off as they pulled out from under the hospital's portico and into traffic.

When they were out of sight, Jenny turned and slowly walked back to the row of chairs. Only one other person was sitting there, reading a magazine. Not in the mood for chance conversation, Jenny perched as far from the woman as she could. Tilting her head back against the wall, she closed her eyes, unutterably weary.

Incredibly, she must have dozed. She awoke with a start when someone spoke her name. Her lids popped up. She blinked, blinded by brightness and trying to recollect her whereabouts.

"Jenny."

It was David's voice, a little weak, a little hoarse. And he was right there in front of her, flat on his back on a gurney, but smiling at her.

"David." She was on her feet and at his side in one swift move. Her eyes took rapid inventory. He was pale, and a large patch had been applied to his forehead. The light blue oxford shirt that was part of the Waterman Aviation uniform lay folded across his hips; his torso above the tan gabardine slacks was bare except for the foot-wide strip of bandaging they'd wrapped around it.

"Does it hurt?" Jenny asked softly, itching to touch him, to hold him, but contenting herself with long looks.

"Only when I laugh." Seeing her worried expression, David tried for a chuckle, grimaced and, with a gasp, added, "See?"

"Don't, David, please." Jenny entreated, feeling his pain as if it were her own. "It's not funny."

"You're right." His eyes, the pupils so dilated they seemed black instead of green, locked onto hers intently. "You've been worried," he said, "and that's not the least bit funny." He caught her hand in his. "You okay?"

"Now I am," she said, fervently returning the pressure of his hand. "Now that I know you are. You are, aren't you?" she added, instantly concerned, when he grimaced again.

"Yes." He squeezed her fingers to reassure her. "I've got a hell of a headache, that's all."

"Soon as we get you in bed, we'll fix you right up." A male nurse walked up and began pushing the gurney up the hall. "You're welcome to walk along, ma'am," he added, and since David still had a hold on her hand, Jenny had little choice but to comply.

"They insist on keeping me overnight," David said disgustedly.

"Concussions can be tricky," the nurse said, maneuvering everybody into an oversize elevator. "No use taking chances."

David pulled a face. "Jenny here'd look after me, wouldn't you, Jen?"

"I'm not much of a nurse, I'm afraid," Jenny said. "I enrolled in a first aid course once, and ended up being the patient."

"What happened?"

"They showed a movie, a car wreck with a bunch of blood. I fainted."

She pulled a wry face; the nurse and David chuckled. Jenny felt terrible when David's little laugh ended in another gasp of pain. "I'm sorry," she said.

The elevator stopped, they all trooped out and up the hall in silence.

"If you'll let go of the lady's hand now, Mr. Waterman, we'll get you settled in this room here," the nurse said, adding to Jenny, "We won't be long, if you care to wait."

"I'll wait."

Just a few minutes later, David was in bed and Jenny perched on the chair next to it.

"I feel ridiculous in this gown," David groused.

"Oh, I don't know." Jenny gave his shoulders and chest in shapeless, faded cotton a teasing once-over. "Looks kinda cute."

David snorted, then wearily closed his eyes. "I must say I'm beat."

"Did he give you something?"

He rolled his head. "No. Not yet. Not sure I want anything."

They were silent a moment. Jenny thought he might have gone to sleep, when he spoke.

"I stopped at Orcas Island today. Checked the cabin."

Her heart began to pound with dread. Orcas. Their weekend. The one she'd decided not to go on with him. "Oh?"

"Everything's all set."

Jenny said nothing. Her mind was in turmoil; she wanted to tell David of her decision, would have already done so if it hadn't been for this....

"It was after I took off from there, cruising along, feeling like the whole world was my oyster, when—zap!—the damn engine and electrical system conked out." He opened his eyes to give her a wry grin. "Talk about a rude return to reality."

"You crashed?"

He grinned again. "I prefer to think of it as a forced landing, albeit not a smooth one."

"The plane?"

"In pretty good shape, considering. Another trawler is towing her in. I can tell you—some heads are gonna roll over this one if shoddy maintenance is to blame. I could've been killed."

"You were lucky."

"Yeah." His gaze snagged hers, and his voice became husky. "Very lucky."

Jenny's heart did a somersault. Now, she told herself, say something now. "David . . ."

"Here's something to make you more comfortable, Mr. Waterman." Another nurse, a young woman, came in carrying a small tray. "If you'll excuse us," she said to Jenny. She set the tray down and began pulling the curtain around the bed. "I'll just give your husband his injection and then you can come back and say goodbye. This'll help him to sleep fairly quickly."

Jenny left the room and paced up and down in the hall, wringing her hands. She *had* to tell him, she thought. Tonight, before she left. He wasn't seriously injured; he was fine, or would be in a day or two. Certainly he himself expected to be, since he intended to go through with their weekend as planned.

Except that she couldn't. Now, after today, after that horrifying self-revelation on her office couch, more than ever she couldn't go.

David's eyes were closed when she came back into the room, but he opened them to drowsily smile at her.

"Hi," he said, "I think they gave me the happy hour special."

She clasped the hand he held out in both of hers. "Sleep's the best thing for you."

"Uh-uh." His lids drifted down. "You're the best thing for me, Jen."

Oh, no, Jenny thought desperately, *please don't say things like that.*

"David," she implored, "there's something I have to say to you...."

"I've got important things to say to you, too." He tried for a wink; his smile so lopsided, it squeezed Jenny's heart.

"David. This is serious." She stopped to take a fortifying breath. "It's about Friday...."

"Hmm..."

"David, I can't go with you to Orcas. I'm sorry."

"Y-you can't?" Frowning, he struggled to open his eyes, to focus on her. "S-something come up?"

"Yes," she whispered. "You could say that."

"I c-could?" He grinned weakly. "Helluva time s-saying anythin'...if you ask me... S'talk tomorrow..." His lids flickered, closed. "'kay?"

His hand in Jenny's went slack.

"Oh, David..." Gently Jenny lowered his arm onto the bed. Reaching out, she stroked his cheek, then leaned down and pressed a light kiss on his slightly parted lips.

"Good night, my love," she whispered hoarsely, her throat on fire with unshed tears. "Goodbye."

Chapter Nine

"I tell you, you can't go in there, Mr. Waterman. Ms. Jones is—"

"Expecting me." The door to Jenny's office was flung wide, framing an enraged David Waterman in its opening.

"Or if she isn't, she oughta be!" he finished with a punishing glare at Jenny, who sat frozen behind her desk. "Tell her," he barked, jerking his head back toward Ruth.

Jenny tore her eyes away from his long enough to give her outraged secretary a reassuring nod. "It's all right, Ruth. Thanks."

With a final, fulminating glare at David's back, Ruth firmly shut the door.

David stayed where he was, a mere foot or two inside the room. His eyes were like emerald laser beams, drilling into Jenny, willing her to look at him. She did, but before she allowed her gaze to become entangled with his, she took quick stock of his person and, with relief, pronounced him whole. No patch on his forehead. Only a fading yellowish discoloration remained to show that two weeks ago there'd been a lump. There was no visible bandaging beneath the thin cotton shirt.

"You look well," she said, willing her voice not to betray the tattered state of her nerves. "Are you feeling all right?"

David didn't answer right away. Something flickered across his face, an expression almost of repugnance, as if he'd just swallowed something bitter. He turned away and walked over to the sofa-and-chair arrangement, but didn't sit. Standing behind the couch, he stared down at one of his fingers smoothing back and forth across the knobby material as if that small act took all of his concentration.

In fact, David needed time out to get a hold of himself, to get control of his emotions and of his voice, which seemed to want to shout harsh recriminations and demands. He hurt, and would rather Jenny didn't know how much.

At length, just when Jenny, increasingly discomfited by David's odd behavior, cast around for something to say, he tilted his head a bit to slant a darkly contemplative, sideways glance at her.

"How do you do that?" he asked, very slowly, almost wonderingly. "How do you manage to look and sound as if you care, when we both know you don't really give a damn?"

"What?" The word was but an incredulous whisper. Jenny was thunderstruck by his preposterous allegation. "How can you say a thing like that after—"

"After *what?*" His control slipping, three strides had David in front of her desk and looming across it. "After what, Jenny? After the caring way you stayed with me at the hospital?"

"You were asleep," Jenny exclaimed, jumping to her feet in agitation only to find that the move brought her face uncomfortably close to his. She shrank into herself without physically pulling back by straightening her spine and folding her arms tightly across her chest. "And Bert Kastell arrived just as I was leaving your room. He said he'd be staying in Anacortes overnight, that in the morning he would be driving you back—"

"And, of course, you knew I'd prefer *his* company to yours," David interrupted with heavy sarcasm.

"What I *knew*," Jenny hotly hurled back, dropping her arms and clenching her hands into fists, "was that you were all right. That you were well taken care of." She forced herself to draw a calming breath and to moderate her tone. "David, there was nothing more for me to do there."

"*I* needed you there, Jenny." David's eyes fiercely drilled into hers as he said that. "I needed you, and you left me."

Jenny clenched her teeth against a stream of hot denials, but knew, as he would know, that they'd be nothing but excuses. She'd never had any intention of staying overnight there with him, none. The reason she'd driven out to Anacortes in the first place was because she hadn't been able to stand the idea of idly waiting for news. Once she knew David was alive, she'd had to make sure he wasn't seriously hurt. And then she'd had to tell him goodbye.

She loved him. David, on the other hand, merely liked and desired her. He had liked and desired enough women in his lifetime, however, to expect a certain number of rejections. He'd survived them all quite nicely, and he would survive this one, too. Right now his pride, his male ego, was wounded by her apparent change of heart, but he'd get over it.

The question was, would *she?*

"I was needed back here, too," Jenny said. It took a supreme effort to keep her gaze level and her tone convincing in spite of the pain in her chest. "I have a responsibility to my business."

"You also had a responsibility to me, yet you not only left Anacortes without a word, you disappeared from the scene altogether," David shot back. "We had a date...."

"Which I told you I wouldn't be able to keep."

"In the hospital! You told me when I was half-looped from that injection, for crying out loud."

"You heard and understood perfectly."

"I said we'd talk about it the next day."

"David, please." Jenny knew it wouldn't take much more for her to come unraveled. "This isn't solving anything. Please, just—"

Her shoulders drooped, and she looked down at her desk with a helpless shake of her head.

"Go?" David quietly finished for her. "Is that what you were going to say, Jen. Please just go? Get out of my life? Scram?"

His voice cracked on the last word, and he violently jerked upright from his crouch across Jenny's desk.

"Is that what you were hoping to accomplish with that disappearing act you pulled these last two weeks, to get rid of me? Is it?"

"No!" Jenny blazed. "At least not entirely. I had unfinished business in Washington—"

"You had unfinished business here."

"I wrote you in my letter—"

"Ah, yes, the letter." He pretended to think. "Let's see, how did it go? Something to the effect of, 'Dear David, on second thought I find I don't want to be your friend, and the idea of becoming your lover no longer does anything for me, either.' Wasn't that it?''

"You know it wasn't." At the bitterness in his voice, Jenny was out from behind her desk in a flash. "David, you know that's not what I—''

"Leave it," he snapped, jerking his arm away from her tentative touch. "What difference do the words make? The message is what counts. And I guess here, today, I finally got your message loud and clear."

"David, please," Jenny entreated. "I wish you'd understand...."

"Understand?" he asked incredulously. "Understand what, for God's sake? That I've been a fool?" His short laugh was scornful. "It took me a while, but I guess I got that message, too."

He stalked to the door. About to wrench it open, his hand on the handle, his gaze on it, too, he stopped. "Why, Jenny?"

He had spoken so softly, Jenny almost didn't hear. Almost. Her heart broke all over again.

"I..." She faltered.

"Why did you bid at the auction, why the pretense of warming toward me—" David almost choked on the burrs stuck in his throat, burrs that painfully ripped and clawed at his vocal chords. "Why did you let me fall in love with you, Jenny, if you never wanted..."

He hesitated as some terrible suspicion dawned, then whirled to face her. He scanned the ghostly pallor of her face and saw in her eyes anguish, guilt and... truth.

"Oh, my God," he whispered. "Russell."

Jenny stood unmoving. What could she say?

"You still think I killed him. You never forgave me."

Still she couldn't speak. After all, it was herself she couldn't forgive.

"Revenge," David whispered, and the pain in his voice tore Jenny's insides to shreds. "If you could make me fall for you, then you could hurt me the way you think I hurt you."

No! Jenny was shaking her head now. She wanted to cover her ears, wanted to shout, *You're wrong! You're wrong!*

But she said nothing. Guilt—oh, Lord, the weight of the guilt she'd kept buried in the darkest recesses of her memory until another tragedy had called it forth! The guilt, the knowledge that at that awful time years ago she hadn't thought of Russell, her lifelong playmate, her truest of friends, she had thought instead of his friend, the man who'd seemed to haunt and taunt her day and night, and hoped he might be alive.

The guilt choked her and locked her in a prison of silence so that no words would come out.

"Well." Looking at Jenny's averted face, David felt mired in defeat. There was nothing else to say, he thought, except to grant her victory. And so he said, his voice rough and his throat sore from that persistent burr he seemed to have swallowed, "You've made me love you, Jenny. Your revenge is complete. I hope it gives you as much joy as I wanted to give you."

Jenny stood without moving as he walked out the door and out of her life. His parting words spiraled through her mind in ever-tightening circles until they coalesced to just a few.

You've made me love you, Jenny... love you, Jenny... love—

She buried her face in her hands and staggered to the couch. Her knees buckled, and she collapsed onto it, bent double, her face still in her hands. There were no tears. The agony and regret at what she had lost was so great that she was beyond them.

Life went on.

Jenny often wondered how, and why, as the summer days grew hotter, and lack of rain sapped the flowers and trees of their vitality just as bouts of depression sapped her of hers. She often told herself that ending her relationship with David had been the right, the *only,* thing to do. That she couldn't have lived with herself if she'd acted otherwise.

So why was it so damn difficult to live with herself now?

It's better this way, was another tack she tried during the course of rationalizations. Friendships, the platonic variety, had never been in the cards for her and David, anyway. Something, perhaps it was that nebulous chemistry Georgette set such stock by, had always been tripping them up.

Sure, she could admit to having briefly flirted with the idea of letting something more between them happen—until she'd realized that she'd been so rash as to let her heart become involved.

She loved him. But that wasn't all.

Lord help her, ever since that horrifying revelation of the day of his accident, when she'd relived the nightmare of that other fateful, life-altering crash, she'd known that she had loved David for a long, long time.

Long enough to make everything she'd claimed to feel for Russell a lie.

Worse, loving David all those years while telling herself and everyone who cared to listen that she despised him, made her entire life a charade. A lie.

She despised herself for all of it but mostly for what she considered to be her betrayal of the love and trust Russell had given her. In the final analysis, it was to atone for that betrayal and to avoid compounding it at all cost, that she'd ended her relationship with David before things got completely out of hand. To have taken that final step, to have made love with David as, heaven knows, she still longed to do with every fiber of her being, would have been the ultimate betrayal of Russell's faith in her.

She was weak. So weak that almost daily, and whenever David's words—I love you, Jenny—echoed in her heart, she longed to go to him and beg him for another chance. She was so weak that if she had continued to see David, been with him, talked and laughed with him, there would have come the moment when her love and need for him would have overridden her principles, and her tortured conscience would have ceased to matter.

And afterward, when it had ended, as it ultimately would have had to end, she would have hated not only herself, but David, too.

It was better this way.

She was used to living alone. She was content to be single. She had a thriving business. She had friends, more friends than she cared to deal with in her current mood. Which only served to emphasize the folly of romantic entanglements, didn't it? She could have spared herself all this heartache if she'd kept to her long-established, tried-and-true code of conduct. She wouldn't now be almost daily rebuffing, antagonizing and offending her friends.

Thank God for her work.

The knock on the door was almost instantly followed by it opening and Ruth sticking her head in. Jenny held up a silencing finger and refocused on the call from New York City she had on the speakerphone.

"And I'm pleased that Herr Baumgartner is pleased, Justin," she said, motioning Ruth to sit down on the chair in front of her desk. "Translating *Dämmerungsträume* into English was a challenge, to say the least." Exchanging wry glances with Ruth, she added, "I'll look forward to his next project."

"Good," Justin Newman boomed. "Then you'll be glad to know it's already written. A spin-off. And getting raves in European literary circles, I might add."

"A spin-off." Jenny covered her eyes with a stifled groan. "How nice."

"Yes," Newman concurred with her facetious remark. "Baumgartner felt that Johannes—the shepherd, remember?—should have his own story...."

Jenny listened to the editor's enthusiastic outline with only half an ear. If it weren't for the money and for the hope of future, more enjoyable work from this publishing house, she would tell Newman to find himself another translator for that demented author's latest scribblings. A story for Johannes... *Give me a break!* Even the sheep that man so ineptly herded were more interesting characters than he.

She glanced at Ruth again and intercepted an unguarded look of concern on the older woman's face. Good old Ruth, Jenny thought with a sigh. Throughout the weeks of heartache, loneliness, self-doubt and soul-searching, she'd been a brick. She knew something was very wrong between Jenny and David, of course, how could she not? She'd seen him storm into Jenny's office that day, and she'd witnessed his subdued departure. Yet not once had she intruded on Jenny's privacy to the point of asking questions. She had merely been more helpful than usual and had put up with Jenny's periodic black moods with grim good humor.

As soon as she decently could, Jenny wound up the call.

"Did you catch that?" she exclaimed, severing the connection. "That lunatic Baumgartner—"

"Wrote a sequel. I got it," Ruth said dryly, rising. "Lucky you."

Jenny's eyes reprimanded, but her lips twitched as she countered with an equally arid, "Thanks, I'm sure. Maybe *you'd* like to do the assignment when it arrives?"

Ruth snorted. "This is one time when I'm grateful I'm only good at fracturing my own language. By the way," she added, as though it were an afterthought, "Robin Lesser of Lesser and Associates called a few minutes ago to make an appointment with you."

"All right." Lesser was an up-and-coming attorney who courted an international clientele. He'd given Jenny's firm quite a lot of work lately.

"Let's see..." Jenny reached across the pile of work on her desk and pulled the calender closer " ...this is Tuesday. Hmm." She flipped a couple of pages. "I can see him Thursday at—"

"I already told him you'd be free today," Ruth interrupted. She glanced at her watch as she walked to the door. "In about ten minutes, to be exact."

"What!" Jenny was on her feet, glaring. "Have you lost your mind? I'm up to my ears, for heaven's sake. What's the matter with you?"

That seemed to be the opening Ruth had been waiting for. "Nothing is the matter with me," she said calmly, unperturbed by her employer's outburst. "Which is more than I've been able to say for you lately. Now, our Mr. Lesser is very eligible, not a pauper, and a very nice man.

He's also recently divorced, probably lonely, and definitely taken with you."

Ruth opened the door. "Do us both a favor and go out with him."

"I don't want to!" Jenny exclaimed, not sure which outraged her more, Ruth's high-handed rearranging of her schedule or the implied reprimand with regard to her behavior of late. "And even if I did," she added, "he's never even asked me."

"He will," Ruth countered, "with a little encouragement. Give it to him."

"But I don't want to," Jenny repeated mulishly. Scowling, she tossed her pencil on the open calender and plopped herself down on the chair. "Ruth, I'm not interested in going out with Robin Lesser. Or any man, for that matter."

"Force yourself. It'll do you good."

Jenny stared at her. "You won't give up," she said incredulously, "until I say I'll do it, is that it?"

"Listen, you don't get to my age, widowed with four kids, by giving up. And neither should you. You're thin as a rail—let Lesser take you to dinner."

"Another mother, that's all I need," Jenny groused. She was truly touched by Ruth's concern, but knew better than to show it. "So I've lost a few pounds—" She shrugged. "It's fashionable to be thin."

"You used to be thin, now you're gaunt. If you ask me, it doesn't suit you."

And with that Ruth firmly shut the door, only to right away open it again.

"Mr. Lesser to see you, Ms. Jones."

Jenny silently vowed revenge as she rose and pasted a smile of welcome onto her face.

"Robin, it's good to see you again." She moved around her desk and indicated the conversational corner. "Shall we sit over there?"

She caught the gleam in the man's eyes and realized with extreme discomfort that Ruth was right. The man's interest in her did seem to exceed mere business. She studied him discreetly as he made his way to the easy chair and settled himself into it while she did likewise across from him.

As a client, Lesser was a jewel. He regularly brought her work, never asked the impossible and promptly paid his bills.

As a man, too, there was little for which Jenny could fault him. He was tall, always a plus when a woman stood five foot ten in her stocking feet, as Jenny did. He dressed beautifully, having been blessed with the kind of unmuscled frame on which even off-the-rack suits would have looked great. Tailor-made suits looked even better, Jenny had to admit. He had a pleasant face and manner, was charming, erudite, obviously sophisticated.

Yet all Jenny could think as she studied him was, If he's so gosh-darn wonderful, why did his wife divorce him?

"Another dynamite contract for us to translate, Robin?" she asked pleasantly.

"Well, actually not." His self-effacing grin displayed two dimples to their best advantage. "I realize I'm being most unprofessional in coming here under false pretenses, Eugenie, but the fact is, I very much need a classy date for a very important dinner this coming Saturday."

"Really?" Good client or not, Jenny had trouble keeping the frost out of both her expression and her voice.

"Yes," he assured her passionately, leaning forward as if to add impact to his words. "And I immediately thought of you." He smiled, sort of winked in a way that had Jenny sitting up straighter. "I need that ice-princess quality you have for this one, babe...."

It was the "babe" that did it, Jenny later told herself, knowing she would always despise herself for not telling him precisely where he could put that patronizing, chauvinistic appellation.

"What night were you thinking, Robin?" she asked coolly, keeping up the pretense she'd been taught—good manners no matter what insulting thing anyone said. Well brought up young ladies didn't voice any naughty rebuttals, her mother had told her many times.

Hey, and well brought up young ladies probably didn't feel inside the way Jenny felt whenever David Waterman teased and taunted her. Excited, hot, *alive.*

"Saturday," Robin said. "This coming Saturday." He smiled. "There aren't a lot of women like you around anymore, Eugenie."

Something told Jenny it might be best not to ask what kind of woman that was, especially since she'd already made up her mind that a date with Robin Lesser was out of the question. She hoped her smile conveyed a regret she was far from feeling.

"Saturday," she said, "what a shame." She'd been invited to go to the opera with Georgette and Bill, but until that moment hadn't been sure she wanted to go. Now she was sure. "I'm afraid I already have a previous commitment."

"Oh?" Lesser had the gall to look doubtful. "With anyone I know?"

"Dr. Faust," Jenny said, a little devil pricking her. "Have you met him?"

"Faust." Robin frowned. "No, I don't believe I have. What's his specialty?"

With an inward rolling of the eyes, Jenny thought, Oh, brother!

Chapter Ten

It was several days later, a Wednesday, and another of Jenny's lunches with Georgette. Conversation between them was desultory, mostly because Jenny was given to long, absentminded silences or monosyllabic replies.

"All right," Georgette snapped finally, after yet again waiting in vain for an answer. "I've had it. Either you tell me what's on your mind, Eugenie Jones, or I'm out of here."

Georgette's sharp tone startled Jenny from her thoughts. "I'm sorry...." She blinked. "You were saying?"

Georgette rolled her eyes. "I've had more satisfying conversations with my dog than I'm having with you lately. At least Trixie pays attention."

"I'm sorry—"

"And will you quit being so gosh darn sorry all the time," Georgette railed. "Especially for yourself!"

"You're angry with me." It occurred to Jenny that she'd never seen her friend so incensed. She touched Georgette's arm. "If I've offended you in some way—"

"Don't you dare say you're sorry."

"All right, I won't." With difficulty, Jenny forced her thoughts away from the myriad regrets that were robbing her life of joy. "But tell me what I said to make you mad."

Georgette jerked her face aside with an inelegant little snort, then turned back to look at Jenny for a long, silent moment. "Jenny, are we friends?"

"Well, of course—"

"Good friends?"

"I thought so, yes...."

"Then for heaven's sake will you talk to me!" After a quick, apologetic glance at their nearest neighbors, Georgette added in a fierce whisper, "Let me help, will you?"

Jenny fielded several interested glances from adjacent tables with a weak, uncomfortable smile. She disliked being an object of public scrutiny almost as much as she abhorred being the recipient of her friend's pity. "Why does everybody think I need help?"

"Because you're acting like a walking wounded," Georgette countered. "Besides, I'm hardly everybody."

"No, you're just a *busybody*," Jenny said, grimacing when her meager attempt at humor got her no more than a quelling glance. She sighed, but her breath audibly caught in the process and she quickly compressed her lips to stifle it.

"All right." Georgette obviously felt it was time to charge in where someone with more tact might have feared to tread. "I've watched you play the martyred soap opera heroine long enough, and, frankly, repetition hasn't made your performance any more appealing to me."

"Well." Jenny drew back as if she'd been slapped. "Thank you very much, *friend*." Hurt and outraged, she fumbled for her purse and started to rise.

"Sit."

Shock and disbelief had Jenny obeying.

"David Waterman loves you, Jenny," Georgette said sternly. "Do you love him?"

Jenny sat rigidly glowering. She'd be damned if she'd say one more word to this female Judas across from her.

"Why am I asking?" Georgette went on undaunted. "Of course you do, or you wouldn't be mired in this pathetic weeping willow imitation." She leaned back in her chair and folded her arms. "I'm listening."

"Well, I'm leaving." Jenny scraped back her chair and half rose.

"Sit," Georgette ordered yet again. "It's clear to me you've made a total mess of things and that you need help. I'm here to give it."

Jenny snapped, "As I said, you're a busybody," but she no longer wanted to get up and leave. Mostly because she too was sick of herself, of her attitude, and of moods that seesawed only between low and lower. She cast a chagrined glance at Georgette and scooted her chair close again. "I've been a royal pain, I suppose, in your esteemed opinion."

"People with needlessly broken hearts usually are."

"I resent that," Jenny flared, hurt again. "Dammit, Georgette, you don't have the first idea what this is about—"

"So enlighten me."

For an instant Jenny considered silent pouting. Stalking off, too, crossed her mind, but she knew she wouldn't. She needed to talk to somebody or go mad. Who'd be a better listener than unshockable, unshakable Georgette?

No sooner had she made up her mind than the words gushed forth with all the force of water bursting through a broken dike. She told of Russell, of David, of the unlikely trio they'd been in their day. Much of what she told Georgette, she knew her friend had already learned or surmised in the course of other, similar conversations they'd had, but Jenny felt she needed to make Georgette realize the depth of her devotion to Russell and the extent of her erstwhile antagonism for David.

She told of the circumstances resulting in Russell's death. He and David had been copilots on a lengthy charter. David had lost the toss of the coin and had flown the outbound leg of the trip. After discharging their passengers, Russell had flown the now-empty plane back while David had slept.

Jenny had to swallow repeatedly in order to smooth the knots of emotion in her vocal chords as she added, "When the call came about David's emergency, it was as if it were . . . that first time, with Russell, all over again. I was back in that time, reliving *that* moment. I prayed, Georgette. With everything in me I . . . I prayed, 'Please, God, let *David* be alive . . . .'"

She bit her lip, anxiously searched her friend's expression. "Do you understand what I'm saying?" she asked, when Georgette didn't speak. "When my first thought should have been for Russell, it was for David."

"Should-have-beens always raise their ugly heads after the fact," Georgette mused, patently unperturbed by Jenny's guilty fervor. "Have you noticed that?"

"Georgette, for heaven's sake—"

"No." Georgette's hand sliced the air in a gesture of finality. "*Jenny, for heaven's sake* is what's appropriate here. Did you wish Russell dead," she demanded, "when you prayed for David to be alive?"

"No, of course not, but—"

"Would you have loved Russell any less, mourned his loss any less, if you'd been able to admit to yourself the fact that you were *in love* with David?"

"Admit to myself? Georgette, I had no idea—"

"Oh, yes, you did, Jen, I'll bet you had plenty of ideas where David Waterman was concerned. Except, being the proper lady you told me you were brought up to be, those ideas shocked and alarmed you, didn't they? They were, quote, not nice, unquote, those thoughts and feelings David aroused, and so you clung more tightly to the security of your fondness for Russell, and shoved what David made you feel into the back closet of your brain."

Georgette leaned back. "First thoughts," she added softly after a pause during which Jenny found nothing in Georgette's words with which she could convincingly disagree, "are from the gut, Jen. They reflect our true feelings, the feelings we have before we censor them with should-haves and supposed-tos. You were in love with David. The only person you hurt with your feelings for him is yourself, because you struggled so to constantly deny them."

"Georgette, I thought I hated him...."

"Love, hate—" Georgette shrugged. "They say they're two sides of the same coin, you know that."

"And my feelings for Russell?" Jenny demanded, her head pounding with the conflicts once again unleashed. "What of them? We were engaged to be married!"

"*Engaged* is the operative word here, Jen. And at this point there's no way of knowing if you ultimately would have gone through with the wedding, is there?" They exchanged a long, mutually thoughtful glance before Georgette added, "I'm betting you wouldn't have."

Georgette was right, Jenny thought, finally able to push aside the gilded gauze curtain through which she had viewed her relationship with Russell after his death. She knew now that she wouldn't have, could never have, married him. It would have been like marrying her brother.

She remembered quickly suppressed second thoughts, nebulous longings for romance, for passion of the kind she'd read about in books. The kind that made your pulse race and your mouth go dry—the way David Waterman was able to do by just looking at her.

Out of the dark, cluttered closet in the back of her mind, where guilt had caused her to hide so many things after Russell's death, now emerged the recollection of her rehearsing the speech she planned to make to him. The one that would tell him once and for all that a wedding was out of the question, not just postponed. She'd already postponed their nuptials twice and she knew Russ wouldn't appreciate her doing it again. This time she'd have to face up to her misgivings, and to Russell, and call things off. Give back the class ring he'd put on her finger in lieu of an engagement ring.

Again and again, she had practiced the words in her mind. I love you, Russell. I want to always be your friend. But I can't marry you.

Again and again, too, her wretched cowardice would cause her to postpone the confrontation. And then one day it was too late. He was dead. And a whole new world of guilt opened up to her....

Weary from it all, wanting with all her heart only to be free of that guilt, free to accept and acknowledge the feelings she had for David, Jenny looked at Georgette. "So now what?"

"So now you tell David you love him."

At that, Jenny smiled in spite of her troubled spirit. How simple Georgette could make things sound. "Just like that, huh?"

"Unless you have a better idea, yes."

"I've hurt him terribly."

Georgette nodded. "I know. And now it's time to heal him."

"I doubt he'll let me."

"But you owe it to yourself, and to him, to try."

Jenny said nothing for a while. She was fighting the urge to throw up her hands and toss in the towel, to say I can't. There's nothing I can do. To do the cowardly thing the way she'd always done in the past—not only with others, but with herself, as well.

Hadn't she pushed away her secret doubts and longings because she'd been afraid to be so vulnerable? Wasn't that why she'd clung to Russell, even become engaged to him, because he was the sure, the safe and comfortable choice?

She was a coward.

Wasn't that why she'd made that bid on David at the auction, because she'd wanted him but was too cowardly to be up-front about it? Wasn't it cowardice that prompted her to end their relationship, because she couldn't handle the vulnerability that came with being in love?

She was a coward. Which was why she'd opted for a trip out of town rather than talk with David face-to-face. Why, when he'd come to her demanding an explanation, she'd let him believe she blamed him for Russell's death rather than lay her true feelings before him.

"I've always been such a damned coward," she admitted bitterly. To herself, really, but Georgette had heard.

"Hey, we all are, one way or another," she assured Jenny, and added, "That's why I'm on television, you know."

The incongruity of her remark made Jenny smile again. "Now that makes sense."

"Of course it does," Georgette said blithely. "Don't you know that the more embarrassing and intimate the confession, the more public should be the forum in which to make it? I mean, I've been able to get things off my chest in the course of my show that I'd never have the nerve to tell a soul face-to-face."

Jenny shook her head, chuckling. "You're outrageous."

"What outrageous?" Georgette protested. "It's the premise of every talk show, every kiss-and-tell book. All sorts of people willingly air their obsessions, addictions and afflictions in public every day."

"So what are you suggesting?" Jenny asked with a dawning suspicion. "Surely not—" Her mother would have apoplexy!

"Absolutely," Georgette declared with a toss of her head. "No, hear me out," she added excitedly, clapping a hand over Jenny's mouth to stifle a protest. "We'll do a sequel to the Issues Concerning Today's Woman piece. You'll recall that both of my other guests took the same content-to-be-single stance you did. Except, guess what? They've both tumbled head over heels since that show! Not only that, but Marcie Ingram, the investment banker, is already pregnant and soon to be married! So."

She settled back and smiled like the Cheshire cat while she studied the stunning ruby-and-diamond ring on her finger. "Since I, too, have found true love," she purred, "the focus of this sequel will be that even a nineties woman—career oriented, independent and savvy—neither is, nor wants to be, immune to Cupid's arrow."

Pausing, she directed expectantly raised brows toward Jenny. "So—what do you think?"

Jenny frowned, gesturing helplessly. "Great, but..." She shrugged. "Where do I fit into this picture of bliss?"

Georgette gave her a reassuring pat. "You, my darling, will be the star attraction."

"Oh?" Foreboding lay as heavy against Jenny's chest as the protective bib the dental hygienist laid across it before taking X rays. "Dare I ask how?"

"Of course." Georgette eyed her with satisfaction. "You, my dear, will be the nineties woman who, in front of millions of viewers, will take control of her life by telling her man that she loves him."

Jenny soon learned that exclamations like, "You're crazy," "I refuse," or "I couldn't possibly," didn't mean a thing when Georgette Myerson, the ambitious TV personality, had a vision and the bit in her teeth.

This show would be a hit, Georgette assured her; this show would usurp—at least for that one morning—the opposing channels' offerings, and ratings, because women all over would love what the show—all right, what *Jenny*— had to say.

"Could we just help each other out here?" Georgette demanded when Jenny continued to agonize over it. And Jenny crumbled.

She told herself, however, that the only reason she agreed to do what Georgette asked was that she owed her friend a favor. She even managed to make herself believe it for an hour or so—until she looked in the mirror and caught sight of the gleam of anticipation in her eye. That's when she admitted that she *wanted* to do it.

Coward that she was, there was no way she'd ever be able to just walk over to Waterman Aviation—or to David's house—stare him in the eye and say, *I've been an idiot. I'm crazy about you.*

No way.

It'd be so much easier just to say it on TV.

"Places everybody. Theme music, and counting, ten, nine, eight, seven..."

"What am I doing here? I must've been crazy! Georgette, there is no way on earth I'm going through with this..."

"...four, three, two..."

"Smile, Jenny!"

"...one. Go."

"Good morning, and welcome to another edition of *Timely Topics*. I'm your host, Georgette Myerson, and..."

Yawning, carefully carrying his first cup of coffee of the day, David padded naked through the bedroom en route to the bathroom. In passing, he saw Georgette Myerson smiling at him from the television set in the corner, as she did nearly every morning.

He wryly saluted her image with his mug. "Looking good there, George."

"We have an exciting show for you today," she was saying. "A follow-up of a program we did a few months ago which you might recall dealt with issues of concern to today's woman. The nineties woman..."

"The nineties woman," Dave grumbled sourly, "give me a break." He went into the bathroom to start the shower, then propped a shoulder against the doorjamb, sipping coffee and watching Georgette, while he waited for the water to warm up.

"The nineties woman has the potential as well as the opportunity to make of her life what she will," Georgette said, "not only in her chosen profession but, as you will learn today, in her personal life, too. *Love*, ladies and gentlemen, will be the topic of today's show. Love and the nineties woman. Stay with us, please, because after this brief message we'll be right back with our guests."

David jerked away from the door frame and was at the TV in two strides. Love, he jeered—a damned four-letter word. With a violent twist of the wrist, he switched off the set and headed for the shower.

An hour later he marched through the doors of Waterman Aviation, his mood black. Which was nothing new, since lately the color of his temper rarely rose above gray. What was new, however, was the fact that he snarled at the hapless receptionist in his front office just because she stared at him with wide eyes and a silly sort of expectant grin on her face.

"What?" David barked, stopping in his tracks to glare at her.

"N-nothing," she stammered, visibly shaken. "I just thought—"

"I pay you to work, not to think," David thundered and, oblivious to the raised brows and perplexed glances being exchanged by the rest of his staff, stomped off toward his office.

He slammed the door behind himself, then leaned back against it and hung his head. "You, Waterman, are a prize jerk."

Exhaling explosively, he pushed away from the door, went to sit behind his desk and picked up the phone. He stabbed a single digit, then drummed his fingers impatiently as he waited for the receptionist to answer.

When she did, he said briskly, "Martha. I'm sorry I snapped at you. A bad morning. All right? What?" He rolled his eyes. "No, dear, not because of something I saw on TV. *Jeez.*" He slammed down the phone, "The woman must think I'm as hooked on soaps as she is."

The monthly financial statements were on his desk to be gone over, and, having duly apologized to Martha, he dismissed the incident from his mind. Going over the figures in front of him, he ought to be rejoicing. Revenues were up, receivables were coming in, his liabilities were in healthy balance with his assets.

Business was good, so if he had the sense he'd been born with, David thought with fervent self-loathing, he'd be a happy man.

Unfortunately, however, in spite of all he had going for him, a happy man he wasn't. He hoped to be again, and soon, but for now all of his once shiny dreams had grown tarnished with neglect because dreaming was something he didn't do much anymore.

His dreams for the house had faded, and summer was marching to a close without seeing the deck and spa he'd planned completed.

He and Sly had taken the boat out a time or two, but, much to the cat's disgust, they hadn't fished.

He never drove the 'Vette these days at all. And all because of a woman.

No, not just *a* woman, that was the trouble. He'd never mope like this, *mourn* like this, if that was the case. He never had in the past. Sure, breaking up had caused him sleepless nights before, had made him question his worth before, and had even made him want to cry or to hit something before—for a few days. And then the fun of the chase, or work, or just life itself would grab him by the throat and shake him out of it.

With a savage oath, David shoved the papers aside and jumped to his feet. Prowling his office like a caged bear, he thought why the *hell* couldn't he shake himself out of it this time? What made this woman special? Not her looks, not her brains, not her walk, her talk, her laughter...

One arm against the wall, David slowly tipped his head forward until it came to rest on it. It was *all* of those things, he thought, wearily closing his eyes. All of those things and more were what made Storky Jones special to him.

He loved her—he'd been hit by that fact just seconds before his plane had hit the drink—but he ought to hate her for what she was putting him through. Yet he couldn't hate her. At least, not yet.

The phone rang, and for the next few hours David's work was able to make him move beyond his misery. One of the instructors was off sick, so David taught a few flight classes that day. One of the students, barely sixteen, brought to the lesson all the eager enthusiasm David and Russ used to have, and David envied him.

The day went swiftly and it wasn't until he climbed into the van at the end of it that David remembered the Daltons were expecting him for dinner. They had called only the day before, and he'd accepted out of habit rather than anything else. He wished now he hadn't. Briefly he debated if he should phone them and cancel. But in the end, knowing Bea would give him an argument, it seemed easier just to go.

As always, Bea was beaming as she opened the door for him. "Davey," she said warmly. "How are you, hon?" Her keen blue eyes searched his face as she caught his hand and drew him inside. "You look terrible."

David kissed her cheek. "I love you, too."

"Well, gosh sakes," Beatrice blustered, leading the way toward the kitchen and Frank. "I would have thought that after—"

She faltered, visibly thrown off balance by something. Her gaze locked with Frank's as David shook hands with him and prompted, "After what, Bea?"

"After such a sunny day you'd be feeling more cheerful," she finished awkwardly, her eyes still linked with her husband's in silent communication. "Frank. Weren't you having trouble with that VCR again? Maybe Davey here could have another look at it."

David slung an affectionate arm across the older man's shoulders, amused by what he knew to be Frank's legendary ineptitude with technical instruments of any kind.

"Lead me to 'er," he quipped, "and maybe afterward you'll give me a beer. What's the problem with it?"

"Well . . ." Frank seemed at a loss. He looked back at Bea.

"We, uh, we recorded something," she said quickly, "and now we can't get it to play."

"Something stuck, is that it?"

"Hmm," went Frank, hunkering down next to David in front of the living room television.

David switched on the set, likewise the VCR, selected the proper channel, hit Play. The screen flickered but stayed blank.

"Okay," David murmured, then reached up to turn on a light. "Well," he said, able to see better now, "the tape's rolling. See, Frank, you can tell by the numbers tallying along right here."

He pointed to the counter, and Frank, looking solemn, nodded his comprehension.

"So," David continued, hitting Stop and then Rewind, "I'd say your only problem was that you hadn't rewound the tape yet. Which isn't a problem at all. See?" To demonstrate, he pressed Stop again, followed by Play, and sat back on his heels to watch.

Georgette Myerson's laughing image filled the screen. "...even I found true love," she was saying, and then she was flashing her ring for all to see. "Isn't this just too gorgeous for words?"

"This is the show you taped?" Dave said with an incongruous little laugh as he surged to his feet. "When I heard this morning what today's topic was, I couldn't shut the set off fast enough...."

He turned to leave the room. "Just hit Stop, Frank," he instructed, "and then Rewind. You've only got the tail end of the show on the screen right now."

"I'm sure you all remember Eugenie Jones..." Georgette's voice accompanied David's exit. "The lady who claimed to be oh, so contentedly single on our previous show. Well, ladies and gentlemen..."

David's step lagged, his eyes met Bea's challenging ones across the hall.

"Have you seen this, Davey?" she asked quietly.

David shook his head.

"Then go watch the tape, son." Bea said.

But David stayed where he was.

"Jenny, too, has succumbed to Cupid's arrow, except that her fella is as yet unaware of his great, good fortune. However, Jenny is with us today to change that, aren't you, Jen?"

"Yes."

Jenny's voice, soft as cotton and husky with emotion, vibrated against David's eardrums like a siren's call. Slowly he turned toward it.

Jenny's face was in close-up, and the sight of her stole David's breath. Her sun-shot hair softly framed her classic features and flowed across her shoulders in waves. Her brows arched gracefully above eyes the color of pansies.

Her nose was proud, the shape of her mouth inviting, her lips slightly parted and curved in a smile.

She looked directly into the camera, directly at *him*, David thought, and he stood as if hypnotized by her steady regard. And then she spoke.

"David," she said, "remember how you once made me promise I'd tell you why I bid on you at the auction, just as soon as I'd figured it out? Well, it took a while—mostly because I'm stubborn and not nearly as smart as you're always telling me I am—but I finally figured it out."

Her smile wobbled and she visibly swallowed before she went on. "It's because I'm crazy in love with you, David Waterman..."

She said other things, but only Bea and Frank Dalton, misty-eyed, were there to hear them.

David was out of the house and in his car, revving the engine and reversing out of the Dalton driveway on squealing tires. He pushed the staid minivan to the limit and his luck to the hilt, but made it into the parking lot of Jenny's building in record time and without getting a ticket.

Too impatient to mess with the elevator, he stormed up the one flight of stairs, and a minimum of long strides brought him to the door of her apartment. He pounded on it with maximum force.

"Storky," he yelled, "I want to see you, and I want to see you now!"

Jenny opened the door. And then just stood there.

David seemed to have spent all of his energy during the fifteen minutes it took him to get to this point, because now that Jenny was in front of him, within easy reach of the arm still poised in midair for knocking, he too seemed immobilized.

They looked at each other. After the initial jolt of eye contact, their gazes raced up and down each other's body as if taking stock or staking claims. And then they homed in on each other's face once again. As if magnetically drawn, their eyes came to rest on each other's lips.

"Hi."

Jenny watched David's mouth form the word, felt it leave his lips and fly to her, and she envied it. She wanted to be that word, only she wanted to fly to *him* and put her lips where the word had been.

And so she did. One step, two, and then one more brought her chest to chest with the man she loved. A slight forward motion of the head, a tiny tilt, and their lips were touching, soft and feather light.

And then with a needy groan, David caught her lips in the desperate heat of his. His arms closed around her like bands of steel and anchored her to him as if for all time.

Their kiss was instantly deep, and though it went on endlessly, for them it seemed all too brief. The sound of footsteps from behind David's back reminded them that they were standing in a well-lit hall.

They drew apart, but only their mouths. And only for as long as it took David to walk Jenny backward across the threshold into the privacy of her apartment. His lips were already back on hers by the time his heel connected with the door and forcefully kicked it shut.

This time the kiss was less urgent, less hungry, less out of control. This time they savored, their tongues stroked and explored, and so did their hands.

Jenny strained to be ever closer to David. Her hands moved across his back, surged up to grip his hair, only to slide back down to tautly muscled buttocks so that she might urge his hips against hers. She wanted him, needed

him against her, and more. She felt the same needs in him
and wanted to cry with the strength of her relief, her joy.

David loved her still. He wanted her still. Her public
declaration had not—as she feared it might have—come
too late.

David, too, felt like a man reborn. A man who'd been
given a second chance at happiness with the only woman
he would ever love. And who loved him. His heart raced,
lifted, turned somersaults in his chest at the knowledge,
and he pulled her more tightly against him as his body
pounded and ached with the need to forever make her his.

He drew back, just a little. Just enough to allow him to
speak. "Tell me, Jen," he roughly whispered.

They were so close, he could see flecks of silver floating
and shimmering in china-blue eyes that passion had dark-
ened to almost navy. He could feel every beat of her heart
as if it came from within himself, and inhaled her breath
as his own while he gave her his.

"I love you, David," Jenny said, her eyes growing ever
darker, wider, the silvery flecks like stars that whirled and
swirled and beckoned for David to drown himself in the
fathomless depth of her adoring gaze.

"Oh, Jen. Sweetheart . . ." His kiss, at once tender and
fierce, touched Jenny's very soul. His words, hot, urgent—"I love you. Oh Lord, I love you so"—made her
tremble. Made her long to—

"No." With a strength born of guilt and the need to be
understood and forgiven, Jenny tore her lips from his and
herself out of his embrace.

She stepped back a pace and, panting as if she'd just run
a marathon, made herself meet the passion-clouded turbulence of David's gaze. He too was panting. His hands
were fists at his side, and he was eyeing her with the same

predatory intensity with which Sly, the cat, eyed his dinner.

"Come back here," he growled, and took a step toward her.

"Not until we've talked," Jenny said, palms up in front of her like shields, and backing away.

"To hell with talk." David advanced another step, then another, while Jenny kept backing up.

His devilish grin should have warned her, but by the time it registered, she had already walked into the back of the couch and was being hurled over it in a slick, one-armed tackle.

They came to rest in a tangle of arms and legs, faces close, bodies much closer. David's grin had gone from devilish to smug. "Good to know the old jock's still got what it takes, isn't it, Stork?" His eyes went to Jenny's lips and the smile faded. "Kiss me, Jen."

Jenny sucked her lips inside her mouth and vehemently shook her head. "Uh-uh."

He moved his hips against hers, his eyes never leaving her mouth. "Love me."

"Hmm..." She nodded but kept her lips compressed.

"Marry me."

"Oh, Da—" Jenny's response was cut short in the sweetest, most satisfying way.

"We need to talk," she gasped, when he finally came up for air.

"Why?" David's lips grazed her jaw, moved up to her ear with gossamer touches that heated Jenny's blood like the finest wine.

"We're both Pisces."

"So?"

"I—" The tip of his tongue invaded her ear, and her breath caught. "Oh, David please..."

"Yes?" He breathed kisses along her temple, her hairline.

"Two Pisces together aren't always compatible—"

"Says who?"

"According to Georgette—"

"To hell with Georgette." David lowered his lips to hers. "Kiss me, Storky."

Jenny did, quickly, then breathlessly insisted, "There's more, though. There's something else I need to explain."

"About Russell?" He gently kissed each delicate eyelid, shaped her brows with the brush of his tongue.

"Y-yes..." Jenny was melting like ice cream beneath the heat of his flickering tongue.

"Did you love him?"

"You know I did, David, but—" Now her other ear was getting its due, and Jenny knew that at this rate she wouldn't be coherent much longer. She wrestled her arms out from beneath the press of David's body, reached up and, firmly gripping the sides of his face, forced it around till their eyes met.

"But I never loved him the way I love you. David, please," she whispered fervently when he would have gone back to more pleasurable pursuits. "I need to say this to you."

In the face of Jenny's vehement intensity, David capitulated. It'd be best to let her get everything she felt she needed to tell him off her chest so that they could finally get past all this talk to some serious action. To be honest, too, he was deeply touched by her struggle to overcome her inherent reticence and bare her soul. Jenny kept her feelings locked up much of the time, just as he did; she bestowed them like precious gifts on only a few. Knowing he was finally one of those few made him feel blessed and content to wait a little longer for the moment when she would finally be his.

"Tell me," he said, putting all of his love into the tone of his voice.

"That day you ditched the plane in the sound," she said softly, "was the day I realized I'd been in love with you for almost as long as I'd known you."

"What?" David tucked in his chin and drew back so he could see her better.

"It's true. And it was scary."

"But the spitfire act all those years, the way you turned from me at the funeral—"

"Defense mechanisms. Coward is my middle name."

"No, darlin'." David lowered his face, rubbed his nose against hers, then lifted his head once more. There were no teasing lights to brighten the greenness of his eyes now, only a rekindling passion and a wealth of love.

"Coward *was* your middle name. What you did this morning on that television show took guts. You saved my life, Jen—"

"My own life, too, David."

He kissed her. "Never leave me again, Storky."

"I won't." Jenny's smile wasn't quite steady, and neither was her voice. "Storky Jones is back in town, and in your life, to stay."

"Storky *Waterman*," David corrected, then looked away, frowning. "Doesn't quite have the same ring to it, does it?"

Jenny pulled his face back to hers, kissed his lips. "You'll get used to it," she whispered.

And he did.

* * * * *

LOVE AND
THE PISCES MAN....

by Wendy Corsi

Whether March comes in like a lion or a lamb, the adventurous Pisces man will undoubtedly be itching to put work aside and get away from it all. A true romantic at heart, this generous fellow will want to treat the special woman in his life to the spring vacation of her dreams. Before the month is over, they'll be enjoying time out for two... and falling in love all over again!

You met fellow Pisceans David Waterman and Eugenie Jones in Storky Jones Is Back in Town. This happy couple is sure to celebrate their upcoming birthdays vacationing near the water—swimming, sailing... or fishing! What will the Pisces man have in store for you?

Intuitive Pisces knows his restless *Aries* mate will be positively bursting with pent-up energy after a long winter. She'll be thrilled when he sweeps her away to a rustic dude ranch for a few days. Riding the trails can be exhilarating, but even the active Aries woman needs to relax sometimes... and she'll delight in cuddling by the campfire with her sensual Pisces man!

Both the Pisces man and the *Taurus* woman delight in self-indulgence... and they'll pamper themselves this spring with a week in Spain! This sensual duo will soak up the sun on the sandy Mediterranean beaches, feast on paella, flan and fine Spanish wine, then romance the night away to the seductive rhythms of the flamenco guitar.

Paris in springtime is perfect for the Pisces man and his mercurial *Gemini* woman. This romantic, vibrant city will satisfy their every mood. They'll spend mornings on whirlwind sight-seeing tours, afternoons people watching at sidewalk cafés... and nights gazing at the stars—and each other—atop the moonlit Eiffel Tower!

Chances are the Pisces man and *Cancer* woman won't care where they go... as long as they're together. But this sentimental duo—both water signs—will naturally be drawn to the deserted rocky seashore of Maine. They'll walk on the empty beach, watch the waves crash in, breathe the fresh salt air... and revel in the absolute solitude of their cozy cottage hideaway by the sea.

The Pisces man knows his fiery *Leo* lady loves a holiday with sizzle, and island-hopping in the Caribbean is definitely hot, hot, hot! They'll romp in the surf all day, and when the sun goes down, the party will begin! The Leo woman can be counted on to lead the conga line and win the limbo contest... but eventually, her romantic Pisces man will lure her away for some slow dancing on a moonlit ocean shore.

No one in the zodiac sign is more organized than the efficient *Virgo* woman, and the Pisces man knows exactly the vacation that will please her most—one that's been planned right to the last detail! She'll be in her element at a spectacular resort where fun-filled activities fill the agenda. From breakfast at dawn to cocktails at dusk, this busy couple will be on the go...but there'll be plenty of time scheduled for love!

The *Libra* woman loves beautiful clothes, and the Pisces man will surprise her with a shopping spree she'll never forget...in Manhattan! He'll insist she splurge on the latest Fifth Avenue styles—his treat, of course—and after each fast-paced day, the thoughtful Pisces man will pamper his weary Libra lady with a chauffeured limousine back to the hotel for a late-night dinner, a soothing bubble bath and a champagne nightcap!

The emotional, dramatic *Scorpio* woman and the intense Pisces man thrive on passion! This March, he'll take his sexy soulmate to exotic Tahiti, where inhibitions are cast aside and sensuality reigns. The pounding island drums and lush tropical backdrop will set the perfect mood for what this enraptured couple has in mind...day and night!

The *Sagittarius* woman's fantasy will come true this spring when she and her romantic Pisces man set sail on a luxury cruise! The outgoing Sagittarian will revel in the shipboard social scene, and when the music starts, she'll be first on the dance floor...in her Pisces man's arms! When the ship sails into a port of call, this extravagant pair will indulge to their hearts' content—in souvenirs, food and lots of togetherness!

As far as the financially savvy *Capricorn* woman is concerned, spring means tax time, and splurging on an expensive trip is out of the question. But the Pisces man knows how to impress her practical side and appeal to her nostalgic nature. Baseball games, bicycle rides and picnics in the park will bring back the good old days when coffee was a nickel . . . and a man still proposed on bended knee!

The free-spirited *Aquarius* woman wants to save the world—and the least the supportive Pisces man can do is help her to explore it! Spring is just the time for this adventuresome team to leave their workaday lives behind and embark on that global journey they've always dreamed about. They're determined to go to the ends of the earth for—and with!—each other.

NORA ROBERTS

Love has a language all its own, and for centuries, flowers have symbolized love's finest expression. Discover the language of flowers—and love—in this romantic collection of 48 favorite books by bestselling author Nora Roberts.

Starting in February, two titles will be available each month at your favorite retail outlet.

In March, look for:

Irish Rose, **Volume #3**
Storm Warning, **Volume #4**

In April, look for:

First Impressions, **Volume #5**
Reflections, **Volume #6**

Collect all 48 titles and become fluent in

THE LANGUAGE of LOVE

The Case of the
Mesmerizing Boss
DIANA PALMER

Diana Palmer's exciting new series,
MOST WANTED, begins in March with
THE CASE OF THE MESMERIZING BOSS....

Dane Lassiter—one-time Texas Ranger
extraordinaire—now heads his own group of
crack private detectives. Soul-scarred by
women, this heart-stopping private eyeful
exists only for his work—until the night his
secretary, Tess Meriwether, becomes the target
of drug dealers. Dane wants to keep her safe.
But their stormy past makes him the one man
Tess *doesn't* want protecting her....

Don't miss THE CASE OF THE MESMERIZING
BOSS by Diana Palmer, first in a lineup of
heroes MOST WANTED! In June, watch for THE
CASE OF THE CONFIRMED BACHELOR...only
from Silhouette Desire!

SDDP-1

MOST WANTED

Silhouette Special Edition

is pleased to present

A GOOD MAN WALKS IN
by Ginna Gray

The story of one strong woman's comeback
and the man who was there for her, Travis McCall,
the renegade cousin to those Blaine siblings,
from Ginna Gray's bestselling trio

FOOLS RUSH IN (#416)
WHERE ANGELS FEAR (#468)
ONCE IN A LIFETIME (#661)

Rebecca Quinn sought shelter at the hideaway on Rincon
Island. Finding Travis McCall—the object of all her childhood
crushes—holed up in the same house threatened to ruin the
respite she so desperately needed. Until their first kiss . . .
Then Travis set out to prove to his lovely Rebecca that man
can be good and love, sublime.

You'll want to be there when Rebecca's disillusionment turns
to joy.

A GOOD MAN WALKS IN #722

Available at your favorite retail outlet this February.

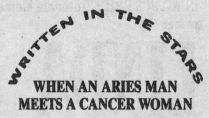

From the popular author of the bestselling title
DUNCAN'S BRIDE (Intimate Moments #349)
comes the

LINDA HOWARD

COLLECTION

Two exquisite collector's editions that contain four of
Linda Howard's early passionate love stories. To add
these special volumes to your own library, be sure
to look for:

VOLUME ONE: *Midnight Rainbow*
Diamond Bay
(Available in March)

VOLUME TWO: *Heartbreaker*
White Lies
(Available in April)

 *Silhouette Books*®

SLH92